JOHN
UPDIKE

FRIENDS FROM
PHILADELPHIA
AND OTHER STORIES

PENGUIN BOOKS

PENGUIN BOOKS

Published by the Penguin Group. Penguin Books Ltd, 27 Wrights Lane, London w8 5TZ, England. Penguin Books USA Inc., 375 Hudson Street, New York, New York 10014, USA. Penguin Books Australia Ltd, Ringwood, Victoria, Australia. Penguin Books Canada Ltd, 10 Alcorn Avenue, Toronto, Ontario, Canada M4V 3B2. Penguin Books (NZ) Ltd, 182–190 Wairau Road, Auckland 10, New Zealand · Penguin Books Ltd, Registered Offices: Harmondsworth, Middlesex, England · 'Friends from Philadelphia', 'Sunday Teasing' and 'The Persistence of Desire' have been taken from *John Updike: Forty Stories*, 'The Other Woman' from *Trust Me* and 'Brother Grasshopper' from *The Afterlife*, published by Penguin Books in 1987, 1988 and 1996 respectively. This collection, selected by Penguin Books, published 1995 · Copyright © John Updike, 1959, 1962, 1985, 1994. All rights reserved · The moral right of the author has been asserted · Typeset by Datix International Limited, Bungay, Suffolk. Printed in England by Clays Ltd, St Ives plc · Except in the United States of America, this book is sold subject to the condition that it shall not, by way of trade or otherwise, be lent, re-sold, hired out, or otherwise circulated without the publisher's prior consent in any form of binding or cover other than that in which it is published and without a similar condition including this condition being imposed on the subsequent purchaser · 10 9 8 7 6 5 4 3 2 1

CONTENTS

Friends from Philadelphia

In the moment before the door was opened to him, he glimpsed her thigh below the half-drawn shade. Thelma was home, then. She was wearing the Camp Winniwoho T-shirt and her quite short shorts.

'Why, my goodness: Janny!' she cried. She always pronounced his name, John, to rhyme with Ann. Earlier that vacation, she had visited in New York City, and tried to talk the way she thought they talked there. 'What on earth ever brings you to me at this odd hour?'

'Hello, Thel,' he said. 'I hope – I guess this is a pretty bad time.' She had been plucking her eyebrows again. He wished she wouldn't do that.

Thelma extended her arm and touched her fingers to the base of John's neck. It wasn't a fond gesture, just a hostess-like one. 'Now, Janny. You know that I – my mother and I – are always happy to be seeing you. Mother, who do you ever guess is here at this odd hour?'

'Don't keep John Nordholm standing there,' Mrs Lutz said. Thelma's mother was settled in the deep red settee watching television and smoking. A coffee cup being used as an ashtray lay in her lap, and her dress was hiked up so that her knees showed.

'Hello, Mrs Lutz,' John said, trying not to look at her broad, pale knees. 'I really hate to bother you at this odd hour.'

'I don't see anything odd about it.' She took a deep-throated drag on her cigarette and exhaled through her nostrils, the way men do. 'Some of the other kids were here earlier this afternoon.'

'I would have come in if anybody had told me.'

Thelma said, 'Oh, Janny! Stop trying to make a martyr of yourself. Keep in touch, they say, if you want to keep up.'

He felt his face grow hot and knew he was blushing, which made him blush all the more. Mrs Lutz shook a wrinkled pack of Herbert Tareytons at him. 'Smoke?' she said.

'I guess not, thanks a lot.'

'You've stopped? It's a bad habit. I wish I had stopped at your age. I'm not sure I even *begun* at your age.'

'No, it's just that I have to go home soon, and my mother would smell the smoke on my breath. She can smell it even through chewing-gum.'

'Why must you go home soon?' Thelma asked.

Mrs Lutz sniffled. 'I have sinus. I can't even smell the flowers in the garden or the food on the table any more. Let the kids smoke if they want, if it makes them feel better. I don't care. My Thelma, she can smoke right in her own home, her own living-room, if she wants to. But she doesn't seem to have the taste for it. I'm just as glad, to tell the truth.'

John hated interrupting, but it was close to five-thirty. 'I have a problem,' he said.

'A problem – how gruesome,' Thelma said. 'And here I thought, Mother, I was being favored with a social call.'

'Don't talk like that,' Mrs Lutz said.

'It's sort of complex,' John began.

'Talk like what, Mother? Talk like what?'

'Then let me turn this off,' Mrs Lutz said, snapping the right knob on the television set.

'Oh, Mother, and I was listening to it!' Thelma toppled into a chair, her legs flashing. John thought when she pouted she was delicious.

Mrs Lutz had set herself to give sympathy. Her lap was broadened and her hands were laid palms upward in it.

'It's not much of a problem,' John assured her. 'But we're having some people up from Philadelphia.' He turned to Thelma and added, 'If anything is going on tonight, I can't get out.'

'Life is just too, too full of disappointments,' Thelma said.

'Look, is there?'

'Too, too full,' Thelma said.

Mrs Lutz made fluttery motions out of her lap. 'These Philadelphia people.'

John said, 'Maybe I shouldn't bother you about this.' He waited, but she just looked more and more patient, so he went on. 'My mother wants to give them wine, and my father isn't home from teaching school yet. He might not get home before the liquor store closes. It's at six, isn't it? My mother's busy cleaning, so I walked in.'

'She made you walk the whole mile? Poor thing, can't you drive?' Mrs Lutz asked.

'*Sure* I can drive. But I'm not sixteen yet.'

'You look a lot taller than sixteen.'

John looked at Thelma to see how she took that one, but 3

Thelma was pretending to read a rented novel wrapped in cellophane.

'I walked all the way in to the liquor store,' John told Mrs Lutz, 'but they wouldn't give me anything without written permission. It was a new man.'

'Your sorrow has rent me in twain,' Thelma said, as if she was reading it from the book.

'Pay no attention, Johnny,' Mrs Lutz said. 'Now Frank will be home any time. Why not wait until he comes and let him run down with you for a bottle?'

'That sounds wonderful. Thanks an awful lot, really.'

Mrs Lutz's hand descended upon the television knob. Some smiling man was playing the piano. John didn't know who he was; there wasn't any television at his house. They watched in silence until Mr Lutz thumped on the porch outside. The empty milk bottles tinkled, as if they had been nudged. 'Now don't be surprised if he has a bit of a load on,' Mrs Lutz said.

Actually, he didn't act at all drunk. He was like a happy husband in the movies. He called Thelma his little pookie-pie and kissed her on the forehead; then he called his wife his big pookie-pie and kissed her on the mouth. Then he solemnly shook John's hand and told him how very, very happy he was to see him here and asked after his parents. 'Is that goon still on television?' he said finally.

'Daddy, please pay attention to somebody else,' Thelma said, turning off the television set. 'Janny wants to talk to you.'

4 'And *I* want to talk to *Johnny*,' Thelma's father said. He

spread his arms suddenly, clenching and unclenching his fists. He was a big man, with shaved grey hair above his tiny ears. John couldn't think of the word to begin.

Mrs Lutz explained the errand. When she was through, Mr Lutz said, 'People from Philadelphia. I bet their name isn't William L. Trexler, is it?'

'No. I forget their name, but it's not that. The man is an engineer. The woman went to college with my mother.'

'Oh. College people. Then we must get them something very, very nice, I should say.'

'Daddy,' Thelma said. '*Please.*The store will close.'

'Tessie, you hear John. People from college. People with diplomas. And it is very nearly closing time, and who isn't on their way?' He took John's shoulder in one hand and Thelma's arm in the other and hustled them through the door. 'We'll be back in one minute, Mamma,' he said.

'Drive carefully,' Mrs Lutz said from the shadowed porch, where her cigarette showed as an orange star.

Mr Lutz drove a huge blue Buick. 'I never went to college,' he said, 'yet I buy a new car whenever I want.' His tone wasn't nasty, but soft and full of wonder.

'Oh, Daddy, not *this* again,' Thelma said, shaking her head at John, so he could understand what all she had to go through. When she looks like that, John thought, I could bite her lip until it bleeds.

'Ever driven this kind of car, John?' Mr Lutz asked.

'No. The only thing I can drive is my parents' Plymouth, and that not very well.'

'What year car is it?'

'I don't know exactly.' John knew perfectly well it was a 1940 model. 'We got it after the war. It has a gear shift. This is automatic, isn't it?'

'Automatic shift, fluid transmission, directional lights, the works,' Mr Lutz said. 'Now, isn't it funny, John? Here is your father, an educated man, with an old Plymouth, yet at the same time I, who never read more than twenty, thirty books in my life . . . it doesn't seem as if there's justice.' He slapped the fender, bent over to get into the car, straightened up abruptly, and said, 'Do you want to drive it?'

Thelma said, 'Daddy's asking you something.'

'I don't know how,' John said.

'It's very easy to learn, very easy. You just slide in there – come on, its getting late,' John got in on the driver's side. He peered out of the windshield. It was a wider car than the Plymouth; the hood looked wide as a boat.

Mr Lutz asked him to grip the little lever behind the steering-wheel. 'You pull it towards you like *that*, that's it, and fit it into one of these notches. "P" stands for "parking" – I hardly ever use that one. "N", that's "neutral", like on the car you have, "D" means "drive" – just put it in there and the car does all the work for you. You are using that one ninety-nine per cent of the time. "L" is "low", for very steep hills, going up or down. And "R" stands for – what?'

'Reverse,' John said.

'Very, very good. Tessie, he's a smart boy. He'll never own a new car. And when you put them all together, you can remember their order by the sentence, Paint No Dimes Light

Red. I thought that up when I was teaching my oldest girl how to drive.'

'Paint No Dimes Light Red,' John said.

'Excellent. Now, let's go.'

A bubble was developing in John's stomach. 'What gear do you want it in to start?' he asked Mr Lutz.

Mr Lutz must not have heard him, because all he said was 'Let's go' again, and he drummed on the dashboard with his finger-tips. They were thick, square fingers, with fur between the knuckles.

Thelma leaned up from the back seat. Her cheek almost touched John's ear. She whispered, 'Put it at "D".'

He did, then he looked for the starter. 'How does he start it?' he asked Thelma.

'I never watch him,' she said. 'There was a button in the last car, but I don't see it in this one.'

'Push on the pedal,' Mr Lutz sang, staring straight ahead and smiling, 'and away we go. And ah, ah, waay we go.'

'Just step on the gas,' Thelma suggested. John pushed down firmly, to keep his leg from trembling. The motor roared and the car bounded away from the kerb. Within a block, though, he could manage the car pretty well.

'It rides like a boat on smooth water,' he told his two passengers. The metaphor pleased him.

Mr Lutz squinted ahead. 'Like a what?'

'Like a boat.'

'Don't go so fast,' Thelma said.

'The motor's so quiet,' John explained. 'Like a sleeping cat.'

Without warning, a truck pulled out of Pearl Street. Mr

Lutz, trying to brake, stamped his foot on the empty floor in front of him. John could hardly keep from laughing. 'I see him,' he said, easing his speed so that the truck had just enough room to make its turn. 'Those trucks think they own the road,' he said. He let one hand slide away from the steering-wheel. One-handed, he whipped around a bus. 'What'll she do on the open road?'

'That's a good question, John,' Mr Lutz said. 'And I don't know the answer. Eighty, maybe.'

'The speedometer goes up to a hundred and ten.' Another pause – nobody seemed to be talking. John said, 'Hell. A baby could drive one of these.'

'For instance, you,' Thelma said.

There were a lot of cars at the liquor store, so John had to double-park the big Buick. 'That's close enough, close enough,' Mr Lutz said. 'Don't get any closer, whoa!' He was out of the car before John could bring it to a complete stop. 'You and Tessie wait here,' he said. 'I'll go in for the liquor.'

'Mr Lutz. Say, Mr Lutz,' John called.

'Daddy!' Thelma shouted.

Mr Lutz returned. 'What is it, boys and girls?' His tone, John noticed, was becoming reedy. He was probably getting hungry.

'Here's the money they gave me.' John pulled two wadded dollars from the change pocket of his dungarees. 'My mother said to get something inexpensive but nice.'

'Inexpensive but nice?' Mr Lutz repeated.

'She said something about California sherry.'

8 'What did she say about it? To get it? Or not to?'

'I guess to get it.'

'You guess.' Mr Lutz shoved himself away from the car and walked backward towards the store as he talked. 'You and Tessie wait in the car. Don't go off somewhere. It's getting late. I'll be only one minute.'

John leaned back in his seat and gracefully rested one hand at the top of the steering-wheel. 'I like your father.'

'You don't know how he acts to Mother,' Thelma said.

John studied the clean line under his wrist and thumb. He flexed his wrist and watched the neat little muscles move in his forearm. 'You know what *I* need?' he said. 'A wrist-watch.'

'Oh, Jan,' Thelma said. 'Stop admiring your own hand. It's really disgusting.'

A ghost of a smile flickered over his lips, but he let his strong nervous fingers remain as they were. 'I'd sell my soul for a drag right now.'

'Daddy keeps a pack in the glove compartment,' Thelma said. 'I'd get them if my fingernails weren't so long.'

'*I'll* get it open,' John said. He leaned over and pushed the recessed button and after a moment of resistance the curved door flopped down. They fished one cigarette out of the old pack of Luckies they found and took alternate puffs. 'Ah,' John said, 'that first drag of the day, clawing and scraping its way down your throat.'

'Be on the look-out for Daddy. They hate my smoking.'

'Thelma.'

'Yes?' She stared deep into his eyes, her face half masked by blue shadow.

9

'Don't pluck your eyebrows.'

'I think it looks nice.'

'It's like calling me "Jan".' There was a silence, not awkward, between them.

'Get rid of the rette, Jan. Daddy just passed the window.'

Being in the liquor store had put Mr Lutz in a soberer mood. 'Here you be, John,' he said, in a businesslike way. He handed John a tall, velvet-red bottle. 'Better let me drive. You drive like a veteran, but I know the roads.'

'I can walk from your house, Mr Lutz,' John said, knowing Mr Lutz wouldn't make him walk. 'Thanks an awful lot for all you've done.'

'I'll drive you up. Philadelphians can't be kept waiting. We can't make this young man walk a mile, now can we, Tessie?' In the sweeping way the man asked the question there was an energy and a hint of danger that kept the young people quiet all the way out of town, although several things were bothering John.

When the car stopped in front of his house, he forced himself to ask, 'Say, Mr Lutz. I wonder if there was any change?'

'What? Oh. I nearly forgot. You'll have your daddy thinking I'm a crook.' He reached into his pocket and without looking handed John a dollar, a quarter, and a penny.

'This seems like a lot,' John said. The wine must be cheap. His stomach squirmed; maybe he had made a mistake. Maybe he should have let his mother phone his father, like she had wanted to, instead of begging her to let him walk to Thelma's.

'It's your change,' Mr Lutz said.

'Well, thanks an awful lot.'

'Good-bye now,' Mr Lutz said.

'So long.' John slammed the door. 'Good-bye, Thelma. Don't forget what I told you.' He winked.

The car pulled out, and John walked up the path. 'Don't forget what I told you,' he repeated to himself, winking. In his hands the bottle was cool and heavy. He glanced at the label; it read *Château Mouton-Rothschild* 1937.

Sunday Teasing

Sunday morning: waking, he felt long as a galaxy, and just lacked the will to get up, to unfurl the great sleepy length beneath the covers and go be disillusioned in the ministry by some servile, peace-of-mind-peddling preacher. If it wasn't peace of mind, it was the integrated individual, and if it wasn't the integrated individual, it was the power hidden within each one of us. Never a stern old commodity like sin or remorse, never an open-faced superstition. So he decided, without pretending that it was the preferable course as well as the easier, to stay home and read St Paul.

His wife fussed around the apartment with a too determined silence; whenever he read the Bible, she acted as if he were playing solitaire without having first invited her to play rummy, or as if he were delivering an oblique attack on Jane Austen and Henry Green, whom she mostly read. Trying to bring her into the Sunday-morning club, he said, 'Here's my grandfather's favourite passage, First Corinthians eleven, verse three. "But I would have you know, that the head of every man is Christ; and the head of the woman is the man; and the head of Christ is God." He loved reading that to my mother. It infuriated her.'

A mulish perplexity occupied Macy's usually bland features. '*What*? The head? The head of every man. What does "The head" mean exactly? I'm sorry, I just don't understand.'

If he had been able to answer her immediately, he would have done so with a smile, but, though the sense of 'head' in the text was perfectly clear, he couldn't find a synonym. After a silence he said, 'It's so obvious.'

'Read me the passage again. I really didn't hear it.'

'No,' he said.

'Come on, please. "The head of the man is God . . ."'

'No.'

She abruptly turned and went into the kitchen. 'All you do is tease,' she said from in there. 'You think it's so funny.' He hadn't been teasing her at all, but her saying it put the idea into his head.

They were having a friend to the midday meal that Sunday, Leonard Byrne, a Jewish friend who, no matter what the discussion was about, turned it to matters of the heart and body. 'Do you realize,' he said half-way through the lamb chops, a minute after a round of remarks concerning the movie *Camille* had unexpectedly died, 'that in our home it was nothing for my father to kiss me? When I'd come home from summer camp, he'd actually em*brace* me – physically embrace me. No inhibitions about it at all. In my home, it was *nothing* for men physically to show affection for one another. I remember my uncle when he came to visit had *no* inhibitions about warmly embracing my father. Now that's one thing I find repugnant, personally re*pugnant*, to me about the American home. That there is none of that. It's evident that the American male has some innate fear of being mistaken for a homosexual. But *why*, that's the interesting thing, *why* should he be so protective of his virility? Why 13 shouldn't the American father kiss the American son, when it's done in Italy, in Russia, in France?'

'It's the pioneer,' Macy said: she seldom volunteered her opinions, and in this case, Arthur felt, did it only to keep Leonard from running on and on and eventually embarrassing himself. Now she was stuck with the words 'It's the pioneer,' which, to judge from her face, were beginning to seem idiotic to her. 'Those men *had* to be virile,' she gamely continued, 'they were out there alone.'

'By the way,' Leonard said, resting his elbow on the very edge of the table and tilting his head towards her, for suaveness, 'do you know, it has been established beyond all doubt, that the American pioneer was a drunkard? But that's not the point. Yes, people say, "the pioneer", but I can't quite see how that affects me, as a second-generation American.'

'But that's it,' Arthur told him. 'It doesn't. You just said yourself that your family wasn't American. They kissed each other. Now take me. *I'm* an American. Eleventh-generation German. White, Protestant, Gentile, small-town, middle-class. I am *pure* American. And do you know, I have never seen my father kiss my mother. Never.'

Leonard, of course, was outraged ('That's shocking,' he said. 'That is truly shocking'), but Macy's reaction was what Arthur had angled for. It was hard to separate her perturbation at the announcement from the perturbation caused by her not knowing if he was lying or not. 'That's not true,' she told Leonard, but then asked Arthur, 'Is it?'

'Of course it's true,' he said, talking more to Leonard than to Macy. 'Our family dreaded body contact. Years went by without my touching my mother. When I went to college, she got into the habit of hugging me good-bye, and now does it whenever we go home. But in my teens, when she was younger, there was nothing of the sort.'

'You know, Arthur, that really frightens me,' Leonard said.

'Why? Why should it? It never occurred to my father to manhandle me. He used to carry me when I was little, but when I got too heavy, he stopped. Just like my mother stopped dressing me when I could do it myself.' Arthur decided to push the proposition farther, since nothing he had said since 'I have never seen my father kiss my mother' had aroused as much interest. 'After a certain age, the normal American boy is raised by casual people who just see in him a source of income – movie-house managers, garage attendants, people in luncheonettes. The man who ran the luncheonette where I ate did nothing but cheat us out of our money and crab about the noise we made, but I loved that man like a father.'

'That's *terrible*, Arthur,' Leonard said. 'In my family we didn't really trust anybody outside the family. Not that we didn't have friends. We had lots of friends. But it wasn't quite the *same*. Macy, your mother kissed you, didn't she?'

'Oh, yes. All the time. And my father.'

'Ah, but Macy's parents are atheists,' Arthur said.

'They're Unitarians,' she said.

Arthur continued, 'Now to go back to your *why* this should be so. What do we know about the United States other than the fact that it was settled by pioneers? It is a   15

Protestant country, perhaps the only one. It and Switzerland. Now what *is* Protestantism? A vision of attaining God with nothing but the mind. Nothing but the mind alone on a mountain-top.'

'Yes, yes, of course. We know that,' Leonard said, though in fact Arthur had just stated (he now remembered) not a definition of Protestantism but Chesterton's definition of Puritanism.

'In place of the bureaucratic, interceding Church,' Arthur went on, trying to correct himself, flushing because his argument had urged him into the sacred groves of his mind, 'Luther's notion of Christ is substituted. The reason why in Catholic countries everybody kisses each other is that it's a huge family – God is a family of three, the Church is a family of millions, even heretics are kind of black sheep of the family. Whereas the Protestant lives all by himself, inside of himself. *Sola fide*. Man *should* be lonely.'

'Yes, yes,' Leonard said, puzzling Arthur; he had meant the statements to be debatable.

Arthur felt his audience was bored, because they were eating again, so he said, as a punch, 'I know when we have kids I'm certainly not going to kiss Macy in front of them.'

It was too harsh a thing to say, too bold; he was too excited. Macy said nothing, did not even look up, but her face was tense with an accusatory meekness.

'No, I don't mean that,' Arthur said. 'It's all lies, lies, lies, lies. My family was very close.'

Macy said to Leonard softly, 'Don't you believe it. He's been telling the truth.'

'I know it,' Leonard said. 'I've always felt that about Arthur's home ever since I met him. I really have.'

And though Leonard could console himself with his supposed insight, something uncongenial had been injected into the gathering, and he became depressed; his mood clouded the room, weighed on their temples like smog, and when, hours later, he left, both Arthur and Macy were unwilling to let him go because he had not had a good time. In a guilty spurt of hospitality, they chattered to him of future arrangements. Leonard walked down the stairs with his hat at an angle less jaunty than when he had come up those stairs – a somehow damp angle, as if he had confused his inner drizzle with a state of outer weather.

Supper-time came. Macy mentioned that she didn't feel well and couldn't eat a bite. Arthur put Benny Goodman's 1938 Carnegie Hall Concert on the record-player and, rousing his wife from the Sunday *Times*, insisted that she, who had been raised on Scarlatti and Purcell, take notice of Jess Stacy's classic piano solo on 'Sing, Sing, Sing', which he played twice, for her benefit. He prepared some chicken-with-rice soup for himself, mixing the can with just half a can of water, since it would be for only one person and need not be too much thinned. The soup, heated to a simmer, looked so nutritious that he asked Macy if she really didn't want any. She looked up and thought. 'Just a cupful,' she said, which left him enough to fill a large bowl – plenty, though not a luxurious plenitude.

'Mm. That was so good,' she said after finishing.

'Feel better?'

'Slightly.'

Macy was reading through a collection of short stories, and Arthur brought the rocking-chair from the bedroom and joined her by the lamp, with his paperback copy of *The Tragic Sense of Life*. Here again she misunderstood him; he knew that his reading Unamuno depressed her, and he was reading the book not to depress her but to get the book finished and depress her no longer. She knew nothing of the contents except for his remark one time that according to the author the source of religion is the unwillingness to die, yet she was suspicious.

'Why don't you ever read anything except scary philosophy?' she asked him.

'It isn't scary,' he said. 'The man's a Christian, sort of.'

'You should read some fiction.'

'I will, I will as soon as I finish this.'

Perhaps an hour passed. 'Oh,' Macy said, dropping her book to the floor. 'That's *so* terrible, it's so *awful*.'

He looked at her inquiringly. She was close to tears.

'There's a story in here,' she explained. 'It just makes you sick. I don't want to think about it.'

'See, if you'd read Kierkegaard instead of squalid fiction –'

'No, really. I don't even think it's a good story, it's so awful.'

He read the story himself, and Macy moved into the sling chair facing him. He was conscious of her body as clouds of pale colour beyond the edge of the page, stirring with gentle unease, like a dawn. 'Very good,' Arthur said when he was done. 'Quite moving.'

'It's so horrible,' Macy said. 'Why was he so awful to his wife?'

'It's all explained. He was out of his caste. He was trapped. A perfectly nice man, corrupted by bad luck.'

'How can you *say* that? That's so ridiculous.'

'Ridiculous! Why Macy, the whole pathos of the story lies in the fact that the man, for all his selfishness and cruelty, loves the woman. After all, *he's* telling the story, and if the wife emerges as a sympathetic character, it's because that's the way he sees her. The description of her at the train – here. "As the train glided away she turned towards me her face, calm and so sweet and which, in the instant before it vanished, appeared a radiant white heart."' The story, clumsily translated from the French, was titled *Un Coeur Blanc*. 'And then later, remembering – "It gladdens me that I was able then to simulate a depth of affection that I did not at that time feel. She too generously repaid me, and in that zealous response was there not her sort of victory?" That's absolutely sympathetic, you see. It's a terrific image – this perceptive man caged in his own weak character.'

To his surprise, Macy had begun to cry. Tears mounted from the lower lids of eyes still looking at him. 'Macy,' he said, kneeling by her chair and touching his forehead to hers. He earnestly wished her well at the moment, yet his actions seemed hurried and morbid. 'What is it? Of course I feel sorry for the woman.'

'You said he was a *nice* man.'

'I didn't mean it. I meant that the horror of the story lies   19 in the fact that the man *does* understand, that he does love the woman.'

'It just shows, it shows how *different* we are.'

'No, we're not. We're exactly alike. Our noses' – he touched hers, then his – 'are alike as two peas, our mouths like two turnips, our chins like two hamsters.' She laughed sobbingly, but the silliness of his refutation proved the truth of her remark.

He held her as long as her crying remained strenuous, and when it relented, she moved to the sofa and lay down, saying, 'It's awful when you have an ache and don't know if it's your head or your ear or your tooth.'

He put the palm of his hand on her forehead. He could never tell about fevers. Her skin felt warm, but then human beings were warm things. 'Have you taken your temperature?'

'I don't know where the thermometer is. Broken, probably.' She lay in a forsaken attitude, with one arm, the bluish underside uppermost, extended outward, supported in mid-air by the limits of its flexure. 'Oog,' she said, sticking out her tongue. 'This room is a mess.' The Bible had never been replaced in the row of books; it lay on its side, spanning four secular volumes. Several glasses, drained after dinner, stood like castle sentries on the window-sill, the mantel, and the lowest shelf of the bookcase. Leonard had left his rubbers under the table. The jacket of the Goodman record lay on the rug, and the Sunday *Times*, that manifold summation of a week's confusion, was oppressively everywhere. Arthur's soup bowl was still on the table; Macy's cup, cockeyed in the saucer, rested by her chair, along with Unamuno and the collection of short stories. 'It's always so awful,' she said. 'Why don't you ever help to keep the room neat?'

'I will, I will. Now you go to bed.' He guided her into the other room and took her temperature. She kept the thermometer in her mouth as she undressed and got into her nightgown. He read her temperature as 98.8°. 'Very very slight,' he told her. 'I prescribe sleep.'

'I look so pale,' she said in front of the bathroom mirror.

'We never should have discussed *Camille*.' When she was in bed, her face pink against the white pillow and the rest of her covered, he said, 'You and Garbo. Tell me how Garbo says, "You're fooling me."'

'You're fooling me,' she said in a fragile Swedish whisper.

Back in the living-room, Arthur returned the books to the shelves, tearing even strips from the *Times* garden section as bookmarks. He assembled the newspaper and laid it on a window-sill. He stood holding Leonard's rubbers for ten seconds, then dropped them in a corner. He took the record off the phonograph, slipped it into its envelope, and hid it in the closet with the others.

Lastly, he collected the dishes and glasses and washed them. As he stood at the sink, his hands in water which, where the suds thinned and broke, showed a silvery grey, the Sunday's events repeated themselves in his mind, bending like nacreous flakes around a central infrangible irritant, becoming the perfect and luminous thought: *You don't know anything*.

The Persistence of Desire

Pennypacker's office still smelled of linoleum. It was a clean, sad scent that seemed to lift from the checkerboard floor in squares of alternating intensity; this pattern had given Clyde as a boy a funny nervous feeling of intersection, and now he stood criss-crossed by a double sense of himself, his present identity extending down from Massachusetts to meet his disconsolate youth in Pennsylvania, projected upward from a distance of years. The enlarged, tinted photograph of a lake in the Canadian wilderness still covered one whole wall, and the walnut-stained chairs and benches continued their vague impersonation of the Shaker manner. The one new thing, set squarely on an orange end table, was a compact black clock constructed like a speedometer; it showed in Arabic numerals the present time – 1.28 – and coiled invisibly in its works the two infinities of past and future. Clyde was early; the waiting-room was empty. He sat down on a chair opposite the clock. Already it was 1.29, and while he watched, the digits slipped again: another drop into the brimming void. He glanced around for the comfort of a clock with a face and gracious, gradual hands. A stopped grandfather matched the other imitation antiques. He opened a magazine and immediately read, 'Science reveals that the cells of the normal human body are replaced *in toto* every seven years.'

The top half of a Dutch door at the other end of the room

opened, and, framed in the square, Pennypacker's secretary turned the bright disc of her face towards him. 'Mr Behn?' she asked in a chiming voice. 'Dr Pennypacker will be back from lunch in a minute.' She vanished backwards into the maze of little rooms where Pennypacker, an eye, ear, nose, and throat man, had arranged his fabulous equipment. Through the bay window Clyde could see traffic, gayer in color than he remembered, hustle down Grand Avenue. On the sidewalk, haltered girls identical in all but name with girls he had known strolled past in twos and threes. Small town perennials, they moved rather mournfully under their burdens of bloom. In the opposite direction packs of the opposite sex carried baseball mitts.

Clyde became so lonely watching his old street that when, with a sucking exclamation, the door from the vestibule opened, he looked up gratefully, certain that the person, this being his home town, would be a friend. When he saw who it was, though every cell in his body had been replaced since he had last seen her, his hands jerked in his lap and blood bounded against his skin.

'Clyde Behn,' she pronounced, with a matronly and patronizing yet frightened finality, as if he were a child and these words the moral of a story.

'Janet.' He awkwardly rose from his chair and crouched, not so much in courtesy as to relieve the pressure on his heart.

'Whatever brings you back to these parts?' She was taking the pose that she was just anyone who once knew him.

He slumped back. 'I'm always coming back. It's just you've never been here.'

'Well, I've' – she seated herself on an orange bench and crossed her plump legs cockily – 'been in Germany with my husband.'

'He was in the Air Force.'

'Yes.' It startled her a little that he knew.

'And he's out now?' Clyde had never met him, but having now seen Janet again, he felt he knew him well – a slight, literal fellow, to judge from the shallowness of the marks he had left on her. He would wear eyebrow-style glasses, be a griper, have some not quite negotiable talent, like playing the clarinet or drawing political cartoons, and now be starting up a drab avenue of business. Selling insurance, most likely. Poor Janet, Clyde felt; except for the interval of himself – his splendid, perishable self – she would never see the light. Yet she had retained her beautiful calm, a sleepless tranquility marked by that pretty little blue puffiness below the eyes. And either she had grown slimmer or he had grown more tolerant of fat. Her thick ankles and the general *obstinacy* of her flesh used to goad him into being cruel.

'Yes.' Her voice indicated that she had withdrawn; perhaps some ugliness of their last parting had recurred to her.

'I was 4-F.' He was ashamed of this, and his confessing it, though she seemed unaware of the change, turned their talk inward. 'A peacetime slacker,' he went on, 'what could be more ignoble?'

She was quiet a while, then asked, 'How many children do you have?'

'Two. Age three and one. A girl and a boy; very symmetrical. Do you' – he blushed lightly, and brushed at his forehead to hide it – 'have any?'

'No, we thought it wouldn't be fair, until we were more fixed.'

Now the quiet moment was his to hold; she had matched him failing for failing. She recrossed her legs, and in a quaint strained way smiled.

'I'm trying to remember,' he admitted, 'the last time we saw each other. I can't remember how we broke up.'

'I can't either,' she said. 'It happened so often.'

Clyde wondered if with that sarcasm she intended to fetch his eyes to the brink of tears of grief. Probably not; premeditation had never been much of a weapon for her, though she had tried to learn it from him.

He moved across the linoleum to sit on the bench beside her. 'I can't tell you,' he said, 'how much, of all the people in this town, you were the one I wanted to see.' It was foolish, but he had prepared it to say, in case he ever saw her again.

'Why?' This was more like her: blunt, pucker-lipped curiosity. He had forgotten it.

'Well, hell. Any number of reasons. I wanted to say something.'

'What?'

'Well, that if I hurt you, it was stupidity, because I was young. I've often wondered since if I did, because it seems now that you were the only person outside my family who ever, actually, *liked* me.'

'Did I?'

'If you think by doing nothing but asking monosyllabic questions you're making an effect, you're wrong.'

She averted her face, leaving, in a sense, only her body – the pale, columnar breadth of arm, the freckled crescent of shoulder muscle under the cotton strap of her summer dress – with him. 'You're the one who's making effects.' It was such a wan, senseless thing to say to defend herself; Clyde, virtually paralyzed by so heavy an injection of love, touched her arm icily.

With a quickness that suggested she had foreseen this, she got up and went to the table by the bay window, where rows of overlapping magazines were laid. She bowed her head to their titles, the nape of her neck in shadow beneath a half-collapsed bun. She had always had trouble keeping her hair pinned.

Clyde's face was burning. 'Is your husband working around here?'

'He's looking for work.' That she kept her back turned while saying this gave him hope.

'Mr Behn?' The petite secretary–nurse, switching like a pendulum, led him back through the sanctums and motioned for him to sit in a high hinged chair padded with black leather. Pennypacker's equipment had always made him nervous; tons of it were marshalled through the rooms. A complex tree of tubes and lenses leaned over his left shoulder, and by his right elbow a porcelain basin was cupped expectantly. An eye chart crisply stated gibberish. In time Pennypacker himself appeared: a tall, stooped man with mottled cheekbones and an air of suppressed anger.

'Now what's the trouble, Clyde?'

'It's nothing; I mean it's very little,' Clyde began, laughing inappropriately. During his adolescence he had developed a joking familiarity with his dentist and his regular doctor, but he had never become intimate with Pennypacker, who remained, what he had seemed at first, an aloof administrator of expensive humiliations. In the third grade he had made Clyde wear glasses. Later, he annually cleaned, with a shrill push of hot water, wax from Clyde's ears, and once had thrust two copper straws up Clyde's nostrils in a futile attempt to purge his sinuses. Clyde always felt unworthy of Pennypacker, felt himself a dirty conduit balking the man's smooth onward flow. 'It's just that for over two months I've had this eyelid that twitters and it makes it difficult to think.'

Pennypacker drew little circles with a pencil-sized flashlight in front of Clyde's right eye.

'It's the left lid,' Clyde said, without daring to turn his head.

'Do you write articles, Clyde?'

'Not usually. I went to a doctor up where I live, and he said it was like a rattle in the fender and there was nothing to do. He said it would go away, but it didn't and didn't, so I had my mother make an appointment for when I came down here to visit.'

Pennypacker moved to the left eye and drew even closer. The distance between the doctor's eyes and the corners of his mouth was very long; the emotional impression of his face close up was like that of those photographs, taken from rockets, in which the earth's curvature was first made apparent. 'How do you like being in your home territory?' Pennypacker asked.

'Fine.'

'Seem a little strange to you?'

The question itself seemed strange. 'A little.'

'Mm. That's interesting.'

'About the eye, there were two things I thought. One was, I got some glasses made in Massachusetts by a man nobody else ever went to, and I thought his prescription might be faulty. His equipment seemed so ancient and kind of full of cobwebs; like a Dürer print.' He never could decide how cultured Pennypacker was; the Canadian lake argued against it, but he was county-famous in his trade, in a county where doctors were as high as the intellectual scale went.

The flashlight, a tepid sun girdled by a grid of optical circles behind which Pennypacker's face loomed dim and colourless, came right to the skin of Clyde's eye, and the vague face lurched forward angrily, and Clyde, blind in a world of light, feared that Pennypacker was inspecting the floor of his soul. Held motionless by fear, he breathed. 'The other was that something might be in it. At night it feels as if there's a tiny speck deep in under the lid.'

Pennypacker reared back and insolently raked the light back and forth across Clyde's face. 'How long have you had this flaky stuff on your lids?'

The insult startled Clyde. 'Is there any?'

'How long have you had it?'

'Some mornings I notice little grains like salt that I thought were what I used to call sleepy-dust –'

'This isn't sleepy-dust,' the doctor said. He repeated, 'This isn't sleepy-dust.' Clyde started to smile at what he took to be kidding of his childish vocabulary, but Pennypacker cut him short with 'Cases of this can lead to loss of the eyelashes.'

'Really?' Clyde was vain of his lashes, which in his boyhood had been exceptionally long, giving his face the alert and tender look of a girl's. 'Do you think it's the reason for the tic?' He imagined his face with the lids bald and the lashes lying scattered on his cheeks like insect legs. 'What can I do?'

'Are you using your eyes a great deal?'

'Some. No more than I ever did.'

Pennypacker's hand, blue after Clyde's dazzlement, lifted an intense brown bottle from a drawer. 'It may be bacteria, it may be allergy; when you leave I'll give you something that should knock it out either way. Do you follow me? Now, Clyde' – his voice became murmurous and consolatory as he placed a cupped hand, rigid as an electrode, on the top of Clyde's head – 'I'm going to put some drops in your eyes so we can check the prescription of the glasses you bought in Massachusetts.'

Clyde didn't remember that the drops stung; so he gasped outright and wept while Pennypacker held the lids apart with his fingers and worked them gently open and shut, as if he were playing with snapdragons. Pennypacker set preposterously small, circular, dark brown glasses on Clyde's face and in exchange took away the stylish horn-rims Clyde had kept in his pocket. It was Pennypacker's method to fill his little rooms with waiting patients and wander from one to another like a dungeon-keeper.

Clyde heard, far off, the secretary's voice tinkle, and, amplified by the hollow hall, Pennypacker's rumble in welcome and Janet's response. The one word 'headaches', petulantly emphasized, stood up in her answer. Then a door was shut. Silence.

Clyde admired how matter-of-fact she had sounded. He had always admired this competence in her, her authority in the world of love in which she was so servile. He remembered how she could outface waitresses and how she would bluff her mother when this watchful woman unexpectedly entered the screened porch where they were supposed to be playing cribbage. Potted elephant plants sat in the corners of the porch like faithful dwarfs; robins had built a nest in the lilac outside, inches from the screen. It had been taken as an omen, a blessing, when one evening their being on the swaying glider no longer distressed the birds.

Unlike, say, the effects of Novocain, the dilation of pupils is impalpable. The wallpaper he saw through the open door seemed as distinct as ever. He held his fingernails close to his nose and was unable to distinguish the cuticles. He touched the sides of his nose, where tears had left trails. He looked at his fingers again, and they seemed fuzzier. He couldn't see his fingerprint whorls. The threads of his shirt had melted into an elusive liquid surface.

30 A door opened and closed, and another patient was ushered

into a consulting-room and imprisoned by Pennypacker. Janet's footsteps had not mingled with the others. Without ever quite sacrificing his reputation for good behavior, Clyde in high school had become fairly bold in heckling teachers he considered stupid or unjust. He got out of his chair, looked down the hall to where a white splinter of secretary showed, and quickly walked past a closed door to a half-closed one. He peeked in.

Janet was sitting in a chair as upright as the one he had left, a two-pronged comb in her mouth, her back arched and her arms up, bundling her hair. As he slipped around the door she plucked the comb from between her teeth and laughed at him. He saw in a little rimless mirror cocked above her head his own head, grimacing with stealth and grotesquely costumed in glasses like two chocolate coins, and appreciated her laughter, though it didn't fit with what he had prepared to say. He said it anyway: 'Janet, are you happy?'

She rose with a practical face and walked past him and clicked the door shut. As she stood facing it, listening for a reaction from outside, he gathered her hair in his hand and lifted it from the nape of her neck, which he had expected to find in shadow but which was instead, to his distended eyes, bright as a candle. He clumsily put his lips to it.

'Don't you love your wife?' she asked.

'Incredibly much,' he murmured into the fine down of her neck.

She moved off, leaving him leaning awkwardly, and in front of the mirror smoothed her mussed hair away from her ears. She sat down again, crossing her wrists in her lap.

'I just got told my eyelashes are going to fall out,' Clyde said.

'Your pretty lashes,' she said somberly.

'Why do you hate me?'

'Shh. I don't hate you now.'

'But you did once.'

'No, I did *not* once. Clyde what *is* this bother? What are you after?'

'Son of a bitch, so I'm a bother. I knew it. You've just forgotten, all the time I've been remembering; you're so *damn* dense. I come in here a bundle of pain to tell you I'm sorry and I want you to be happy, and all I get is the back of your neck.' Affected by what had happened to his eyes, his tongue had loosened, pouring out impressions; with culminating incoherence he dropped to his knees beside her chair, wondering if the thump would bring Pennypacker. 'I must see you again,' he blurted.

'Shh.'

'I come back here and the only person who was ever pleasant to me I discover I maltreated so much she hates me.'

'Clyde,' she said, 'you didn't maltreat me. You were a good boy to me.'

Straightening up on his knees, he fumbled his fingers around the hem of the neck of her dress and tugged it and looked down into the blurred cavity between her breasts. He had a remembrance of her freckles vanishing like melted snow in the whiteness within her bathing suit. His clumsy glasses hit her cheek.

She stabbed the back of his hand with the points of her comb and he got to his feet, rearing high into a new, less sorrowful atmosphere. 'When?' he asked, short of breath.

'No,' she said.

'What's your married name?'

'Clyde, I thought you were successful. I thought you had beautiful children. Aren't you happy?'

'I am, I am; but' – the rest was so purely inspired its utterance only grazed his lips – 'happiness isn't everything.'

Footsteps ticked down the hall, towards their door, past it. Fear emptied his chest, yet with an excellent imitation of his old high-school flippancy he blew her a kiss, waited, opened the door, and whirled through it. His hand had left the knob when the secretary emerging from the room where he should have been, confronted him in the linoleum-smelling hall. 'Where could I get a drink of water?' he asked plaintively, assuming the hunch and whine of a blind beggar. In truth, he had, without knowing it, become thirsty.

'Once a year I pass through your territory,' Pennypacker intoned as he slipped a growing weight of lenses into the tin frame on Clyde's nose. He had returned to Clyde more relaxed and chatty, now that all his little rooms were full. Clyde had tried to figure out from the pattern of noise if Janet had been dismissed. He believed she had. The thought made his eyelid twitter. He didn't even know her married name. 'Down the Turnpike,' Pennypacker droned on, while his face flickered in and out of focus, 'up the New Jersey Pike, over the George Washington Bridge, up the Merritt,   33 then up Route 7 all the way to Lake Champlain. To hunt the big bass. There's an experience for you to write an article about.'

'I notice you have a new clock in your waiting-room.'

'That's a Christmas present from the Alton Optical Company. Can you read that line?'

'H, I, F, Y, T, something that's either an S or an E –'

'K,' Pennypacker said without looking. The poor devil, he had all those letters memorized, all that gibberish – abruptly, Clyde wanted to love him. The oculist altered one lens. 'Is it better this way? . . . Or this way?'

At the end of the examination, Pennypacker said, 'Though the man's equipment was dusty, he gave you a good prescription. In your right eye the axis of astigmatism has rotated several degrees, which is corrected in the lenses. If you have been experiencing a sense of strain, part of the reason, Clyde, is that these heavy frames are slipping down on your nose and giving you a prismatic effect. For a firm fit you should have metal frames, with adjustable nose pads.'

'They leave such ugly dents on the sides of your nose.'

'You should have them. Your bridge, you see' – he tapped his own – 'is recessed. It takes a regular face to support unarticulated frames. Do you wear your glasses all the time?'

'For the movies and reading. When I got them in the third grade you told me that was all I needed them for.'

'You should wear them all the time.'

'Really? Even just for walking around?'

34   'All the time, yes. You have middle-aged eyes.'

Pennypacker gave him a little plastic squeeze bottle of drops.

'That is for the fungus on your lids.'

'Fungus? There's a brutal thought. Well, will it cure the tic?'

Pennypacker impatiently snapped, 'The tic is caused by muscular fatigue.'

Thus Clyde was dismissed into a tainted world where things evaded his focus. He went down the hall in his sunglasses and was told by the secretary that he would receive a bill. The waiting-room was full now, mostly with downcast old men and myopic children gnawing at their mothers. From out of this crowd a ripe young woman arose and came against his chest, and Clyde, included in the intimacy of the aroma her hair and skin gave off, felt weak and broad and grand, like a declining rose. Janet tucked a folded note into the pocket of his shirt and said conversationally, 'He's waiting outside in the car.'

The neutral, ominous 'he' opened wide a conspiracy Clyde instantly entered. He stayed behind a minute, to give her time to get away. Ringed by the judging eyes of the young and old, he felt like an actor snug behind the blinding protection of the footlights; he squinted prolongedly at the speedometer-clock, which, like a letter delivered on the stage, in fact was blank. Then, smiling ironically towards both sides, he left the waiting-room, coming into Pennypacker's entrance hall, a cubicle equipped with a stucco umbrella stand and a red rubber mat saying, in letters so large he could read them, WALK IN.

He had not expected to be unable to read her note. He held it at arm's length and slowly brought it towards his face, wiggling it in the light from outdoors. Though he did this several times, it didn't yield even the simplest word. Just wet blue specks. Under the specks, however, in their intensity and disposition, he believed he could make out the handwriting – slanted, open, unoriginal – familiar to him from other notes received long ago. This glimpse, through the skin of the paper, of her plain self quickened and sweetened his desire more than touching her had. He tucked the note back into his shirt pocket and its stiffness there made a shield for his heart. In this armor he stepped into the familiar street. The maples, macadam, shadows, houses, cement, were to his violated eyes as brilliant as a scene remembered; he became a child again in this town, where life was a distant adventure, a rumor, an always imminent joy.

The Other Woman

Ed Marston awoke in the night to urinate, and as he groped his way back to bed the moonlight picked out a strange flash of white paper in his wife's top bureau drawer, which she had not quite closed. This drawer, he knew from twenty-two years of cohabitation, Carol devoted to her underthings and a small stack of folded headscarves over on the left. Paper belonged in her desk downstairs, or on the hall table, where she usually left the day's mail. She was breathing steadily, obliviously, like an invisible ocean in the dark, not ten feet away. With two fingers extended in a pincer, taking care not to rustle, Ed extracted the paper out from under the top scarf and crept back to the bathroom. He shut the door, turned on the light, and sat on the closed toilet seat. As he unfolded the concealed document, his hands were, more than trembling, jumping.

It was a homemade valentine to her from the husband of a couple they knew, a pleasant bland couple he had never much noticed, on the politer fringes of their acquaintanceship. Yet the valentine had been flamboyantly penned and phrased with a ceremonious ardor, its short text encircled by a large heart in red ink, a heart which, the writer reassured the receiver, was 'even bigger this year than last'.

A weapon had been placed in Ed's hands. He reread the missive more than once, and in his nervous excitement had to lift up the seat and urinate again. He switched off the bathroom light. The moon-struck snow outside the window seemed to leap bluely toward him, into him, with its smooth and expansive curves of coldness, its patches of shadow and glare. He felt toweringly tall, as if his feet rested not on the bathroom floor, which had fallen away, but on the earth itself. His trustfully sleeping wife, and her lover asleep in his house up the road, and that man's own wife, and all their combined children were in his hands.

Still trembling, he refolded the valentine. Sliding along beside the bed toward the bureau in its slant of moonlight, he soundlessly tucked it back into the drawer, beneath the top silk scarf. Tomorrow Carol might notice its slightly exposed position, and rebuke herself, and thank God that Ed had not noticed. Not that she was much one for rebuking herself, or thanking God.

Suddenly her voice, out of the darkness of the bed, asked sharply, 'What are you doing?'

'Trying to find you, sweetie. I've just been to the bathroom.'

She made no answer, as if she had spoken in her sleep. When he got back into the warm bed beside her, her breathing seemed as deep and oblivious as before. Gently the aroma of sleeping flesh and its soft snuffles and rasps washed over his senses. Her life was like a spring in some dark forest, constantly, murmuringly overflowing. Far away in the neighborhood, a dog barked, excited by the moonlight on the snow.

It fit, he realized: Carol's volatile moods of late, her spells of lovingness and depression, her increased drinking, her unexplained lateness in returning from certain trips into New York and from evening meetings in their suburb – meetings of a zoning commission, come to think of it, of which the other man, Jason Reynolds, was the chairman. It had been he, in fact, who had proposed Carol for membership; he had come to the house one night, after a portentous phone call, and, while Ed obligingly did the dinner dishes and put the youngest child to bed, murmured downstairs to her, at the dining-room table, of the crisis facing their suburb, of predatory builders and their corrupt brothers-in-law on the planning board, of the need for a woman on the commission who was here during the weekdays and could bring a homemaker's point of view, and so on. Carol had told Ed all this afterwards, wondering whether she should accept. It would take her out of the home, she worried; Ed told her she had put in enough time in the home. She didn't know anything about planning or building; he told her, speaking as an engineer, that there wasn't much to know.

Now he wondered if even then, over two years ago, the affair had begun and she was only pretending to vacillate, to hang back. If so, it had been a pretty piece of acting. Ed smiled appreciatively in the dark. He had urged her to accept because she had seemed to him in danger of becoming one of those suburban agoraphobes who wind up not daring to leave the house even to shop, who have everything delivered while they sit sipping sherry behind the drawn curtains. Twenty-two years and five children had pretty well absorbed the venturesome subway-rider and semi-Bohemian, in sneakers and babushka, of their city days. She could hardly be persuaded, these last years, to come into town and join him for dinner and a play. Her nervousness about flying, as the children attained college age and began to fly here and there, increased to a phobia, and she no longer felt up to the trips she and Ed used to take to the Caribbean in the winter. 'Anyway,' she would argue, 'they say now the sun is terrible for your skin.' Carol was blue-eyed, with wiggly oak-pale hair.

'It's always been terrible; your skin wasn't meant to last forever. You can sit inside and read. You can use a number-fifteen sun block.'

'Well, that seems to defeat the whole purpose of going. Why not just stay home and save the airfare?'

'You know something, my dear? You're becoming a real drag.' Ed had urged her to accept the commission appointment because he wanted her out of the house. He wanted her, if the truth be known, out of his life.

But she had done him no harm – had done, indeed, everything he had asked. Borne him healthy children, created a home that could be displayed to colleagues and friends, served as an extension of his ego. Yet, lying beside her night after night, rising to urinate once, twice, depending on his insomnia, which expanded in spirals like a rage, he had become convinced that there must be a better life than this. A better life for the both of them. Carol had her qualities still – a flexible grace, though she had put on weight with the years, and a good-humored intuitiveness that was like the

pure blue pilot light burning in an old-fashioned oven – but

Ed had never dared expect that some other man might covet her. Jason Reynolds's message, in its festive red outline, had struck a tone handsomely blended of friendliness and passion, a tone of manly adoration. Carol, somehow, was loved. Realizing this made Ed, too, feel loved, and like a child in arms he fell swiftly asleep.

For days and weeks Ed did nothing with his knowledge, merely observed. How could he not have seen before? At parties, the lovers would do a long circling dance of avoidance, elaborately courteous and jolly with almost everyone else there, and only after dinner, when the shoes come off and the records go on, and the tired host brings fresh logs up from the cellar, did Carol and Jason allow themselves to drift together, and to talk quietly in that solemn way of people to whom the most trivial daily details of one another's lives have acquired the gravity of the sexual, and then to dance together with a practiced tenderness that they trusted those around them to be too drunk or sleepy to observe.

Jason was a thin and dignified man, a trust officer at a midtown bank, who observed a rigorous health regimen of exercise and diet; he had a rowing machine, played squash at lunchtime in the city, and after dinner jogged along the country roads in a reflective orange vest. It sometimes happens with such people that their bodies make their faces pay the price of aging, and so it was with him: his middle-aged face needed flesh. His fatless, taut, weather-yellowed features, his deep eye sockets and long creased cheeks and dry gray hair were those of a man ending rather than beginning his 41 forties. Jason was forty-two, like Carol. In his arms she looked young, and her broad hips suggested a relaxed and rounded fertility rather than middle-aged spread. Though Jason's eyelids were lowered in their deep sockets, and seemed to shudder in the firelight, Carol's blue eyes were alertly round and her face as pristine and blank as a china statuette's each time the slow music turned her around so Ed could see her. It was not their faces that gave it away, it was their hands, their joined hands melting bonelessly together and Jason's other hand pressing an inch or two too low on the small of Carol's back.

Ed was not watching alone, he noticed; the flickering, dim room, cushions and chairs and fuzzy heads and stockinged legs, was lined with shadows watching Jason and Carol, or studiously not watching. People knew – had known, with the casual accuracy of detached observation, long before he had, before the night of the valentine. Until then he had existed in a kind of bubble, a courteous gap in the communal wisdom. He had been blundering with a blind smile through society while the truth, giggling, just evaded his fingertips. This, in retrospect, was hard to forgive. Did his opposite number, Patricia Reynolds, also exist in such a bubble? What did she know, or guess, or feel?

She was a short woman, with exemplary posture, who seemed wooden to Ed. Even her prettiest feature, her thick chestnut hair, seemed a shade of wood, brushed shiny and cut short in a helmet shape, with bangs. She jogged and exercised alongside Jason, but the regimen that had ravaged his face gave hers instead a bland athletic smoothness. Her chin was square, her brown eyes opaque. From a wealthy but not famous family, she had attended correct second-best schools and was thoroughly the product of her background; with a mannish upper-class accent, throatier than one expected, Pat had a good-soldier air about her, as if she had stiffened in her mission of carrying her family line into the next generation. There were two Reynolds children – a son and a daughter. Pat was slightly younger than Jason, as Carol was younger than Ed. Ed had never heard Pat say anything unpleasant or unconventional; but, then, he had rarely listened to her. At parties they tended to avoid each other. He had the feeling that he, with his rumpled, sleepless air, his incorrigible cigarettes and bossy, clownish, perhaps coarse manner, rather dismayed her; when he approached, she grew extra polite. Now, though, his eyes sought out her chiselled profile in the room, to see if she, like him, was watching.

In fact, she was seated on the floor not far away and, her face turned full away from the dancers, was discussing with another woman that most appropriate of topics for the commission chairman's wife, zoning – the tragic break-up of the local estates, the scandalous predations of the developers. Ed moved from his easy chair to the floor near her and said, 'But, baby – you don't mind my calling you "baby", do you, Pat? – nobody wants to *live* in the old estates. The third generation is all in SoHo doing graffiti art. They can't afford the upkeep and the taxes and nobody can afford servants and they want to get their money *out* and in *hand*.'

'Well, of course that's what everybody says,' Pat said, 'and I suppose there's some truth to it.'

'*Some* truth! It's all truth, Pat honey.' Six bourbons were talking through him, not quite in synchrony. 'You blame these poor hard-working Italian contractors who do the bull-dozing and put up their four-hundred-thousand-dollar tract houses, but it's the rich, the *rich* who are greedy, who are dying to sell and let somebody else put the new slate roof on Daddy's old stables. Condominiumization' – he was so proud at having got the word out intact that even Pat smiled, briefly showing her dental perfection – 'is the only way to save these old places from the wrecker's ball.'

The woman next to Pat, Georgene Fuller, tried to come to the rescue. She was lanky and lazy and whiny, with long bleached hair loose to her shoulders. Ed had slept with her, for six months, years ago. 'Still, Ed, you have to admit –'

'I have to admit nothing,' he said quickly. 'How about you, Pat? What do you have to admit?'

A flicker of puzzlement crossed this other woman's even features. Georgene nudged Ed in the small of his back. But she needn't have feared; it suited him to have Pat in the dark, in her bubble.

'The wrecker's ball,' he resumed. 'It should be the name of a song. We're gonna dance off both our shoes,' he began to sing. The pressure on his back repeated, and it occurred to him he should ask Georgene to dance. Once you sleep with them, however many years go by, they fit smoothly into your arms.

But others also wished to break up the conversation be-tween Pat and Ed; Jason and Carol suddenly loomed over them like parents above children playing on the floor. 'We think you two should dance with us,' Carol announced primly, and obliging Ed pushed himself up from the floor, which seemed with the bourbon to have taken on an elastic life of its own, and to bounce under his feet. Carol, rather miraculously, always felt slightly strange in his arms, as though their many years of marriage had never been. They had never quite worked out the steps, and this awkwardness made her interesting, especially now that he knew that somewhere, with somebody else, she *was* working out the steps. Her plump body felt solid with her secret, and unusually flexible to him; reaching behind her gracefully, she adjusted the position of his hand on her back. Ed had experimentally placed it an inch or two lower than usual. 'Jason looks like a smooth dancer,' he said.

'Not that I noticed,' she answered.

'He is with Pat. Look at them go. Twirls, and everything.'

'They went to the same sort of cotillions.'

'But there's more to life than cotillions, huh?'

'Ed, you really shouldn't drink so much. It's what gives you insomnia – all that sugar in the blood.'

'Next you'll be telling me I should take up jogging.'

'Or something. It's not just you. We're *both* horribly out of shape.'

He moved his hand lower again on her back and patted her solid fanny. He had his husband's prerogatives still. 'To me you feel just right,' he said.

Ed was an engineer, specializing in stress analysis of tall steel-frame buildings. His plan for dismantling his marriage demanded that his wife's affair remain in place, as a temporary support; otherwise, at the moment of pullout, his burden of guilt and strangeness would be too much. The children were heaviest, but the house, the town, and all the old connubial habits would weigh upon him in his moment of flight. He feared that Jason and Carol might break up out of their own dynamics, or in response to discovery from the other side; yet he wanted to allow some months to steel himself, as it were. Seeing, in the raw spring evenings, tall Jason moving with his jogger's stagger along the shadowy roads, Ed felt a pang of alarm that the precious man would be hit by a car, and the whole structure collapse.

Warm weather arrived, with its quickening of the blood, and then summer, with its promiscuous looseness, its airy weave of coming and going, of lingering light and warm darkness, of screened porches and reactivated swimming pools and pickup drinks on the patio. Everyone got browner in the summer, more frolicsome and louder; the suburban women in their bathing suits and sundresses took on the sultry hardness of high-class whores – their eyes hidden behind sunglasses, their toenails lacquered. Jason and Carol became more blatant; more than once, Ed spotted them holding hands in a corner of a cocktail party, and when asked where she had been during some unaccountable absence, she would give a teenager's lame, evasive answer – 'Oh, out.' She might add, 'It's so hot I had to take a walk toward the river,' or else display a half-gallon carton of skimmed milk and a packet of wheat-germ cookies as if the purchase of these had naturally consumed two hours. And Jason was always coming around to the house on more or less plausible errands, having to do with zoning or tennis or an exchange of gardening equipment. Ed, to make his tennis-court fence ten years ago, had invested forty dollars in one of those two-handled post-hole diggers, and it was surprising how many posts Jason seemed to be planting in his modest back yard, or how often, for a man who owned only a half-acre, he had to borrow Ed's chainsaw. Every errand, of course, won from Carol a hospitable offer of coffee or tea or a drink, depending on the time of day.

Pat sometimes came along on these hollow excursions, and made flawless, wooden small talk with Ed out on the screened porch while the other two were coincidentally absent within the house: Carol had had to rush into the kitchen, Jason to the bathroom or to make a phone call. The house, that summer, seemed much used. Carol kept setting up, around the excuses of the tennis court and the swimming pool, informal little parties that almost always included the Reynoldses. One day in early August, returning to the house from an emergency run to the liquor store downtown, Ed swung into the driveway as Carol and Jason were greeting another couple. They looked so natural, posed side by side in the golden late-afternoon light, so *presiding*, standing together one flagstone step up from the driveway, he with his gray hair and gaunt stoop and she with her matronly round arms and shoulders, that Ed felt abolished, already gone; he secretly shared their joy in each other, and yet primitive indignation contributed to his energy as he marched toward them with the rattling bags of liquor. Carol looked toward him; she 47 seemed unfeignedly happy to see him. Or was it the liquor she was happy to see? She was wearing only a wrap-around denim skirt over her black bathing suit, and in the chill of approaching evening was hugging herself; the homeyness of this ageless gesture, and the familiar small sight, as she stepped down and reached forward to take one of the bags from him, of the downy hairs standing erect with goosebumps on her bare forearms, wounded him unexpectedly – activated random stress within a situation he had considered thoroughly analyzed.

The season was ebbing. Ed had to make his move. The children were conveniently scattered to summer jobs and to friends' houses, but for the youngest, who after dinner wrapped himself in the mumble of television in his room upstairs. Ed invited Carol to take a walk with him. Her eyes widened, into their china-doll look, and she hurried to get a jacket from the closet; the tone of his voice, without his willing it, had spoken to her guilt. They walked along the broad grassy path, favored by joggers and snowmobilers, kept open above the Croton Aqueduct, which poured water south in a line parallel to the river and the railroad tracks. The city's gravity pulled everything toward it. The Marstons walked uphill, between clumps and groves of maples and beeches, and past school grounds seen through wire fencing; back yards abutted on the right-of-way, and Ed and Carol felt themselves moving like ghosts through family cookouts and badminton games and the domestic music of chugging dishwashers and the evening news.

He described to her the night he had discovered the

valentine, and what he had observed since. She listened and did not interrupt; in the corner of his vision, against the moving background of leaves and fence slats, her pale face seemed a motionless image projected from a slide upon a skidding, flickering screen. He proposed this to her: he would leave, take an apartment in the city, and take her secret with him. In return for his silence, she would present the separation to their children and friends as a mutual decision. He would provide financial support, and in a year they would see how things stood.

She spoke at last. 'I'll give him up.'

'Oh, don't do that.'

'Why not?' Her eyes had grown watery, seeking his.

'You love him.'

'Maybe I love you, too.'

'You think that now, but in the long run . . .' The sentence trailed off. He summoned up a little indignation. 'Anyway, I don't want to be loved *too*. Come on, Carol,' he said. 'We've given it a good try, had some nice kids and nice times; you wouldn't have taken up with Jason if things were what they should be. You and he, you really seem to have it.'

She could have denied it. But she simply said, 'He has Pat.'

Ed sighed. 'Yes, well. I can't take care of everybody.'

This was a Saturday. The next day, with the sickening new condition of their marriage drying everywhere like an invisible paste, and the children and the pets and the furniture all still unknowing, Carol surprised Ed by still wanting to be taken to a Sunday-afternoon concert at a local church. The

Reynoldses were also there, in a pew on the far side of the nave; they all mingled over punch afterwards, in the ladies' parlor. It was thrilling, for a connoisseur of stress, to see Carol lightly bantering with Jason and making valiant small talk with Pat. As Ed drove her home, she began to cry, and he asked her why she had wanted to come. 'It was my only chance to see Jason,' she confessed, as bluntly as if to a counsellor, and not bothering to hide the reverent way her voice fell in pronouncing her lover's name. So quickly, Ed had become her accomplice. He felt his heart shiver and harden. 'He knows I know?'

'Not the details, just the fact.'

'How did you manage that?'

'I slipped a note to him. Didn't you see?'

Ed felt trapped and betrayed. With the other man knowing, there was less chance of backing out. 'No.'

'I thought you'd become such a great observer.'

He asked her, sarcastic in turn, 'Aren't you two afraid of Pat catching you out in some of these shenanigans?'

'She doesn't want to catch us out,' Carol told him. He glanced over, and her eyes, though red-rimmed, had a twinkle. She seemed to be adjusting to his departure faster than he was.

That fall, Ed entered into the strange new status of half-husband. He found a small apartment in the West Eighties and went home weekends to rake and put up storm windows and entertain the kids. Some nights, he slept over in the guest room, where the children didn't like to find him. They wanted him back in Mommy's bed. That creepy Mr Reynolds was always coming around, red-faced and panting, in his jogging shoes. They called him Big Foot. 'Big Foot's just clumped up!' one of the children would shout from downstairs, and Ed, involved in a game of Trivial Pursuit in his oldest daughter's room, would see Carol sail past the door, her quick step silent, her whole body lightened by expectation.

In this cozy atmosphere, with their conspiracy now widened to include the children, Ed asked Carol, in curiosity as much as envy, what Jason did for her that he had not. 'It's very peculiar,' she admitted, spacing her words. 'He just thinks I'm amazingly wonderful.' And she had the grace, this valuation being so clearly excessive, to look down into her drink and blush.

'Well, who doesn't?' he asked, himself blushing. Since leaving her, Ed was all flattery.

She looked up sharply. Did he imagine it, or had her blue eyes become darker, snappier in her months of living alone, of being her own woman? Certainly her hair, its oak color loaded with gray, had become wigglier. '*You* didn't,' she told him. 'You never did. I was just *there* for you, like an I-beam or something. Any other beam would have done just as well. I'm sure you've laid some in place already.'

'No,' he said slowly, almost truthfully. For in fact Ed was enjoying the shabby austerity, the modest purity, of bachelor life. He had married so young he had never had to cook for himself before, or make his own bed. These skills had seemed arcane to him, and now they proved learnable, and 51 he understood why women were healthier, with all that reaching and stirring and industrious attention to the texture of things. His crowded, clamorous, only slightly dangerous block near upper Broadway spoke to him more intimately, of small decisions and services, groceries and laundry, than the suburbs ever had. Keeping himself fed and tidy and half-running Carol's household forty minutes to the north took most of his energy. Living alone makes one methodical; his drinking had eased off, and the weekend slices of his old social life tasted sour and flat.

He had rarely seen their friends except on weekends anyway, and in these days of domestic confusion his defection and part-time re-appearance were casually accepted. The Reynoldses, of the couples they had known together, were kindest and most attentive to Carol in her singleness, and came by the house oftenest. Pat and she shared garden-club trips, aerobics classes, a night course in the English Romantic poets at the local community college. The Marston children gave Pat the logical nickname of Little Foot, as if by verbal magic to knit the Reynoldses closer together. 'The Feet are here again,' one would shout, and Ed, if he was caught in the house, would sometimes have to make a fourth at tennis.

He always insisted that he and Pat be partners. That way, the sides were most even. Jason was a well-schooled but lumbering player, and Carol's insouciance, her good-humored indifference to the exact outcome, undermined her natural grace at the game. Ed had a weak backhand but killer instinct at the net, and little Pat placed, it seemed to him, like a weakly wound-up machine. She moved back and forth as if on tiptoe and her movements minced in the sides of his vision. Across the net from her, Ed would have gobbled up her ladylike forehands and pounded them back at her. As it was, he would growl, 'Let's go get 'em, Pat,' and count on her to cover the back line as he lunged from side to side, looking for the winning volley. The matches were fun, especially when fussy, no-fat-on-me Jason began to tut and mutter to himself, and Carol grew rosy in the face as she tried to play to please her lover while both acknowledging Ed's ironic glances and keeping her expression blank for Pat's benefit.

In a way, it was the three of them against Pat. Or was it the three of them keeping her safe in her bubble of ignorance? Ed felt alternately that they were a deceit machine, chewing her up, and a kind of cradle, holding her above the abyss. For what, really, he asked himself, would telling her the truth have done but force her to act and perhaps plunge them all into disaster? How much did Pat suspect? Nothing, it appeared, which seemed incredible to Ed; just looking at Jason and Carol across the net, hearing their mutual encouragements, feeling the easy warmth their partnership gave off should have told Pat the tale. Once he joked to her, 'You know what they look like, those two? Mr and Mrs Jack Sprat.' It was true: in the stress of their long affair, Jason had become even thinner and Carol plumper. Pat laughed politely but emptily, intent on her serve. Though her strokes lacked fire, she did like to win; this much was human about her, and intelligible, and likable.

She was the youngest, their baby, not quite forty; and Ed, at forty-five, felt like the daddy, only playing at playing. His sense of their spatial relations, out on the court, was of himself enclosing the three others and of keeping them, with transparent lines of force, apart, as if under his direction had been struck one of those balances of gravity and inertia, rigidity and mass that form islands of stability within the universe. Pat's ignorance, he decided, was a function of her social complacence, and thus more annoying than pitiable. She had snobbishly willed herself to be sexually blind.

Only once, that long sunny fall they shared, was he physically stirred by her; after three sets she complained of a blister, and on the bench by the side of the court took off her sneaker and sock. Little Foot. The neatness that through the rest of her body seemed rather wooden and mechanical here in her bare, pale foot was exquisite; here in the long low late-afternoon rays that slanted upon them, imprinting their sweaty bodies and tennis outfits with the fencing's shadowy lozenges, Pat's sharp, small anklebones and metatarsal tendons and unpainted toenails roused in Ed a desire to kneel in slobbering self-abasement and to kiss this tidy white piece of woman, to whose golden sole adhered a few cinnamon-red grains of clay-court topping.

Pat felt his eyes feasting on her foot and looked up as if he were a shoe salesman who had failed to answer a perfectly reasonable question. The moment passed.

'Doesn't she think it strange,' Ed asked Carol, 'always getting stuck with us, always being dragged here?'

'She likes me,' Carol said, with her endearing insouciance. 'She feels sorry for me.'

54   'Does she ever ask why I left?'

'No. Not really. We don't discuss that sort of thing. I think she just sees you as a rather wild, unpredictable person and there's no accounting for what people like you do.'

'As opposed to people like Jason.'

'Mm-hm.' Just thinking of Jason made Carol's lips draw in as though she were sucking a candy.

'What's she going to do when she finds out?'

'I don't know. Ask me to give him up, and I guess I'll have to.'

'Have you ever thought of giving him up right now, before there's an ugly crisis?'

Carol sipped at her drink and reminded him, 'I offered to, and you said no.'

'That was in relation to us. I'm thinking of it now for your sake. Don't you ever feel terribly guilty toward her?'

'All the time,' Carol confessed – rather cheerfully, Ed thought.

'Aren't you ever afraid I'm going to tell her?'

'No. That's the last thing you'd ever do.'

'Why not?'

'Because you're a coward,' she promptly, lightly said, and softened it to 'The same reason nobody tells her – even her own children. They discuss it with mine. Ours. We're all cowards. Anyway, what would be in it for you? You got your exit visa, you don't care what happens to us back in the old country.'

'Oh, but I do. I do. Apparently I wasn't a very satisfactory husband for you. I'm trying to arrange one for you that is.'

'That's very kind of you, dear,' Carol said. Ed couldn't tell   55 if she was being ironic. His deceptions included this ambiguity toward Carol: was he aiming truly to be rid of her or in some circuitous way to win her back – to show her who, underneath all, was boss?

He always boarded the train south, back to his apartment and his block, with some relief to be out of the suburban cat's-cradle he had helped weave. But his life, his life as his reptile brain grasped it, was still back there, witnessing Carol's wifely blushes on the other side of the net and the other woman's exposed bare foot, like the helpless cold foot of a cadaver, in the warm sunset light. Sunday nights, in bed, he could not stop replaying the tennis match, its diagonals and elastic, changing distances. Round watching faces, children's faces in the grandstands – though in fact the children rarely came to watch; they snubbed it all – became frustratingly confused with the fuzzy balls being battered back and forth. Eventually he would fall asleep, with no boundary between insomnia and dream and no healing sense, when he awoke, of having slept soundly. Being alone in bed made even a small room seem large, and reverberant, like a great drum with the ceiling for a skin.

At last, mercifully, the weather became too cold for tennis. He did not want to face Pat anymore, however securely this woman was sealed in her bubble of unknowing. The lovers had come to accept their precarious situation as settled, and Ed's complicity as their right. His role as confidant subtly expanded to that of pander. Carol took to asking, in that casual, irresistible way of hers, if they could borrow his apartment during the day, when he was off at work. Returning through the winter dark, he would find his bed made with an alien neatness, and sometimes a bottle of wine in the refrigerator, or his Martini pitcher used as a vase for a bright bouquet of flowers, the kind of bouquet peddled in a paper cone, at subway entrances or from gloomy traffic islands.

The city was slowly absorbing Ed. He had made a few friends, if not commitments, and asked that on weekends Carol send the children, those young enough still to be interested, in on the train. The echoing halls of the Museum of Natural History welcomed him back from his own childhood; many of the exhibits were jazzier, and pedagogic voices talked from the walls, but the extinct creatures had not aged, and the African dioramas still had the same airless, suspenseful enchantment of Christmas windows along Fifth Avenue. A dry tuft of foreground grass or a few presumably geologically accurate pebbles scattered to lend verisimilitude would fascinate him, as if these humble details, just inches inside the great glass pane, had a secret vitality denied the stiff stuffed creatures at the center of the exhibit. When, late that winter, Pat's bubble at last broke, Ed felt well removed from the crisis, which was muffled by a snowstorm in any case. Carol kept phoning him, and several times a cloud of static overwhelmed her voice, and the connection was broken.

Apparently a maiden aunt of Pat's, who lived in the next town to the south, in one of those big Hudson River houses that had not yet been condominiumized, had seen Jason and Carol in a car together, at eight thirty on a weekday morning. Ed knew it was their habit for Jason to miss the train that Pat   57 had dropped him off to catch, walk a block or two to where Carol would pick him up, and then take the next train from the station farther down the line; in this way they stole a half-hour for themselves. A dangerous habit, and hardly worth it, Ed had advised Carol long ago. But the little wifely act of putting Jason on a train had been precious to her. The aunt, seeing them with dim eyes from her own moving car, had thought Carol must be Pat, but heavier than she had ever seen her, with bushier hair, and the car didn't seem exactly familiar, either; yet there was no mistaking Jason – that long head, thin as a knife. Troubled by the possibility that she was going senile and seeing things, the innocent old lady telephoned to have her vision confirmed.

'Evidently,' Carol told Ed, 'Pat very coolly lied and said yes, she had been taking Jason to a different station because they had dropped off their other car at a gas station near the town line.'

'What she could have said that would have been better,' Ed pointed out, 'was that Jason had accepted a ride that particular morning with a woman they both knew who also commutes. It happens all the time. I assume you were driving the Honda.'

'It needs its snow tires, by the way. I totally forgot to have them put on. I've been nearly getting killed.'

'Then what happened?'

'Well, I guess she stewed all day, but still hoped Jason would have some explanation when he came back. But this image, of a fat woman with messy hair, she instantly con-
58 nected with me. How do you like that for an insult?'

Ed saw Carol's expression as she said this, her self-mocking face, eyes rounded, corners of her lips drawn down. It occurred to him that Pat had been snobbishly unable to believe that he and Carol, messy and clownish as they were, could ever do anything that would matter, seriously, to herself and her husband. 'Well, he's here. I mean, he was here. He's had to go back because she isn't *there*, it turns out.' In a flurry of static, an annoyed operator came on and told them that this line was being pre-empted for an emergency call. In the imposed silence, snow continued to pile up in parallel ridges on the fire escape. The lights of upper Broadway were burning a yellow-pink patch into the streaming sky. An occasional siren could be heard, trying to clear a path for itself, but the city was inexorably filling up with a smothering, peaceable snow. Ed paced back and forth; his hands, as he mixed himself a drink, were jumping. His old calculations were being upheld, miles and miles away.

Carol got through in an hour and continued her story. 'Well, she's apparently left the house. Leaving the two children there. In the middle of this blizzard. It's crazy. Jason is very upset, but I think it's just her rigid way of doing things. She has no sense,' she said, in the pedagogic voice of the experienced woman, 'of riding with the punches.'

'Was her reaction anger, or despair, or what?'

Carol paused before selecting, 'Indignation. She was indignant, first off, that her aunt had been sullied somehow; she thinks that idiotic family of hers is something sacred. Then I guess she was indignant that Jason couldn't come up with a cover story that would get us all off the hook; he says he'd just come off the train after a rotten day at the bank and was too tired to think. So instead he kind of collapsed and told her everything. What really got to her, what she couldn't get over, was how everybody except her had known or guessed about us for years. She kept reliving everything, all these little moments that came back. She had even seen us holding hands a couple of times, it turns out, but couldn't believe her eyes.'

'Was she especially sore at me? It must have come out that I knew, too.'

Carol paused again; Ed felt she was being tactful. 'Not especially. I don't think they discussed you much. I don't want to hurt your feelings, but you're really a very minor figure in all this. It was more the notion of the community at large, of looking like a fool in front of everybody for so long.'

'In her pretty bubble,' Ed said. Carol had been right: he was a coward. For a year he had been dreading the phone call from Pat asking for a conference, asking him what he knew. The call had never come; in her doughty innocence she had never asked, and he had been almost grovellingly grateful to her for that. Perhaps she too had done some stress analysis. Now, evidently, she had stormed out of the house, in the thick of a blizzard. She had cracked. Ed circled the room in his triumph, in his agitation. All night, as the plows on the street kept scraping holes in his sleep, he imagined that Pat, who was missing, would rap on his door. The secret he had so long kept was off his hands, and out whirling in the world. The voice of the wind was her voice, so coolly and multiply wronged. He would comfort her, she would take off her soaked boots and be barefoot, exposing again that little foot so tidily formed and yet somehow in essence immature, a child's foot, ignorant, luminous ... He awoke, and it was morning, and a stark brilliance like that of an offended angel stood at the window. The sky was blank blue, and a hush as of guilt lay everywhere. With scraping shovels and whining tires, the city began to put itself back together.

Pat, it turned out, had done the conventional thing: she had fled to her mother's, on Long Island. 'She drove right across greater New York,' Carol explained to Ed, 'along all these choked highways, through this blinding storm.'

'What an epic,' he said, relieved that Pat was still alive.

'I've been talking to Jason about it,' Carol said, as loosely chatty as if to a psychotherapist, 'and as I told him, I think it was typical. Everything with her has to be black or white; she has no feeling for gray areas.'

Pat never returned to the husband or the town that had deceived her. The teenaged children elected to stay with their schools and friends, which meant that they stayed with their father, which meant that Carol coped. The two households were gradually merged into one. Mothering the wounded and hostile Reynolds children suited Carol's talents better than the zoning commission. In the summer, Jason moved in with her – he had always coveted, Ed thought, their bigger yard, and tennis court, and the stand of woods out back, and the screen of tall arborvitae in front, between the house and the road. The Marston children coined a nickname for their mother: they called her Happy Foot. Pat 61 at her distance disdained the new realities as she had disdained the old; though initially she had all society's sympathy and legal bias on her side, her rigid, vindictive behavior, especially toward her own children (they, too, had known, she maintained, and had kept her in the dark), eroded her advantages, and by the fall Jason's lawyer saw no insurmountable obstacle to achieving divorce and custody, though Pat had vowed to give him neither.

Ed was kept abreast of all this not only through Carol, whose calls gradually became less frequent and less confiding, but through the children and their visits, and through Georgene Fuller, his lanky friend of old, who also paid visits. His interest in the episode lessened, as toward any completed job. His former wife was happy, his children were virtually adult, and the new Mr and Mrs Reynolds (who honeymooned in St Thomas) sent him, when February rolled round once again, a homemade valentine.

On a bright day one April – the squinting, wincing kind when winter's grit is swirled from the city streets and green garbage bags torn by dogs go loping down the sidewalks – Ed saw Pat Reynolds a half-block away. It was an unlikely neighborhood, the West Thirties, to bump into anyone you knew. He was hurrying to a dreaded appointment with his periodontist; he had fallen into the hands of a team of young specialists who were going to give him, in their cheery words, 'a new mouth'. Root canals, refashioned crowns and bridges – but the worst of all was the gum work, with tiny quick knives and sickles and scrapers, by a humming young man who wore a thick gold chain around his neck.

Pat, when Ed thought of her, was another kind of soreness, an ache as if a rib had been long ago removed or as if, that first glaring morning after the snowstorm, the side of him toward the window had been exposed to radiation. In all the world she was the person he least wanted to see. He considered ducking into a jeweler's entryway, or hiding in a store that offered souvenirs to the tourists straggling back from the Empire State Building; but his appointment wouldn't wait, and Pat's face was momentarily turned the other way. She wore a bright red scarf on her head and carried a shopping bag, which, with her sneakers and black raincoat, gave her a forlorn, wandering air. He had the irrational impression that she was in this neighborhood for some sort of medical attention also; she was hesitating right in front of the very entryway, a large mustard-colored arch, that he must pass through to have his gums cut. He had almost slipped by, squinting against the gritty wind, when she turned her head and recognized him.

'Ed! Ed Marston.' Her voice had changed; the suburban little-man throatiness had become warmer, as if she, too, lived in the city now and was learning to deal in its heated, semi-European style. 'Come here,' she commanded, seeing his tendency to keep moving through the arch.

He went to her and she lifted herself on tiptoe to kiss him. The chiselled edges of her face had been blurred; her features had undergone that subtle bloating one sees on the faces of addicts, even when cured. Underneath the scarf her hair was the same rich chestnut, no longer a sleek helmet but unbecomingly permed into curliness. He tried to kiss her cheek but 63 she aimed for the center of his mouth; having pressed her lips hard to one corner of his, she hung on, resting her face on his shoulder a long moment. His brain felt numbed. He asked, 'How've you been?'

'*Good.*' The word was italicized; it must have been a lie, but it was offered with a fervor that would have made it true. She watched his face, waiting for another question, but since none came, asked him, 'And you?'

'Terrible,' he told her, which was also something of a lie. 'I'm going right now to see my periodontist – they do these terrible things to your poor gums.' Clowning in his embarrassment, he grimaced so that his gums showed.

Pat's eyes were solemn, shining. She nodded. Her own gums, of course, would still be perfect. With great relief Ed realized that no accusations or interrogation would be forthcoming; the bubble to that extent was still intact. A bit more small talk, a mock-desperate pointing at his wristwatch, and he had made his grateful escape. He never had had much to say to Pat. A backward glance as he pushed the elevator button showed the red of her uncharacteristic scarf (she had always gone bareheaded, even in the worst of winter, jogging along beside Jason) being sliced and battered on the far side of the revolving door.

Her kiss, so unexpectedly passionate, felt like a visible encumbrance on his mouth. What had it meant? That she had crazily forgotten who he was, and how he had betrayed her? Or that she forgave him? Or that she saw him now as just a piece of the past and had hung on to him a moment as we all wish to hang on to what is gone? Or that – and this fit

64

best, as Ed heard his name called and stood to go in to his punishment – she was in her embrace acknowledging their closeness that night when, in an exultant, trembling moment, he had held her, too, in his hands?

Brother Grasshopper

Fred Emmet – swarthy and thick-set, with humorless straight eyebrows almost meeting above his nose – had been an only child. If he ever fantasized a sibling for himself, it was a sister, not a brother. His father had had a brother, an older brother, who, he let it be known, had dominated him cruelly. Yet into even his more resentful reminiscences crept a warmth that Fred envied, as he tried to imagine the games of catch, decades ago, on the vacant lots of a city that no longer had vacant lots, and the shared paper route in snow that was deeper and more dramatic than any snow today is, with a different scent – the scent of wet leather and of damp wool knickers. Though his father's brother had deliberately thrown the ball too hard, and finished delivering papers to his side of the street first and never came back to help but instead waited inside the warm candy store, a brother was something his father had *had*, augmenting his existence, giving it an additional dimension available to him all his life. 'My brother down in Deerfield Beach,' he would drop into a conversation, or 'If you were to express that view to my brother, he'd tell you flat out you're crazy.' And, though the brothers lived over a thousand miles apart, one in Florida and the other in New Jersey, and saw each other less than once a year, they died within a few months of each other, Fred's father following his older brother as if into one more vacant lot, to shag flies for him.

But this was years later, when Fred's own children were grown, or nearly. He had married early, right after Harvard, supplying himself with another roommate, as it were, rather than launching into life alone. He envied siblings their imagined power of consultation, of conspiring against parents who otherwise would be too powerful. Not the least of the charms his future wife held for him was her sister – a younger sister also at Radcliffe, with her own circle of friends. Germaine was more animated, more gregarious and more obviously pretty than Fred's sensible Betsy. Among her numerous suitors the most conspicuous was Carlyle Saughterfield, a tall bony New Englander with a careless, potent manner.

Fred had been sickly and much-protected as a child, and even his late growth spurt had left him well under six feet tall. He found Carlyle, who was two years older than he and a student at the Business School across the river, exotic and intimidating – a grown man with his own car, a green Studebaker convertible, and confident access to the skills and equipment of expensive sports like sailing, skiing, climbing, and hunting. Carlyle and his B-School friends would load up his snappy green convertible with skis and boots and beer and sleeping bags and head north into snow country with the top down. Details of their mountain adventures made Fred shudder – sheer ice, blinding fog, tainted venison that left them all vomiting, ski trails bearing terrible names like Devil's Head and Suicide Ravine. Climbing in the White Mountains one summer, Carlyle had seen a friend fall, turning in the air a few feet away as Carlyle pressed into the cliff and gripped the pitons.

'What was the expression on his face?' Fred asked.

Carlyle's somewhat protuberant eyes appeared to moisten, as he visualized the fatal moment. 'Impassive,' he said.

His voice, husky and hard to hear, as if strained through something like baleen, was the one weak thing about him; but even this impressed Fred. Back in New Jersey, the big men, gangsters and police chiefs and Knights of Columbus, spoke softly, forcing others to listen.

As their courtship of the Terwilliger sisters proceeded in parallel, Fred and Carlyle spent an accumulating number of hours together. In the spring, waiting for the girls to come out of their dorms, they played catch in the Quad with a squash ball; Carlyle's throws made Fred's hands sting and revived his childhood fear of being hit in the face and having an eye or a tooth knocked out. The strength stored in the other man's long arms and wide, sloping shoulders was amazing – a whippy, excessive strength almost burdensome, Fred imagined, to carry. Carlyle had been a jock at prep school, but in college had disdained organized sports; a tendency to veer away from the expected was perhaps another weakness of his. Behind the Business School, across from Harvard Stadium, a soccer field existed where the future financiers played touch football. Carlyle passed for immense distances, sometimes into Fred's eagerly reaching hands, and protectively saw to it that his timorous and undersized brother in courtship usually played on his team.

In March of the year that Fred and Betsy graduated, the two couples went skiing, and Carlyle was as patient as a

professional instructor, teaching Fred the snowplow and stem christie and carefully bringing him down, at the end of the day, through the shadows of the intermediate slope. All these upper-class skills involved danger, Fred noticed. That summer, after he and Betsy had married, Carlyle took them and Germaine sailing on Buzzards Bay and, while the two sisters stretched out in their underwear for sunbaths on the bow, commanded in his reedy voice that Fred take the tiller and hold the mainsheet – take all this responsibility into his hands!

'Take it. Push it left to make the prow move to the right. The prow's the thing in front.'

'I'd just as soon rather not. I'm happy being a passenger.'

'Take it, Freddy.'

The huge boat leaned terrifyingly under gusts of invisible pressure, the monstrous sail rippling and the mast impaling the sun and the keel slapping blindly through the treacherous water, nothing firm under them, even the horizon and its islands skidding and shifty. Nevertheless, the boat did not capsize. Fred gradually got a slight feel for it – for the sun and salt air and rocking horizon. Germaine's breasts in their bra were bigger than Betsy's, her pubic bush made a shadowy cushion under her underpants as the sisters lazily, trustfully chattered. Carlyle's face, uplifted to the sun with bulging closed eyelids had a betranced look; his colorless fair hair, already thinning, and longer than a businessman's should be, streamed behind him in the wind. *This bastard*, Fred thought, as the boat sickeningly heeled, *is trying to make a man of me*.

When, the following summer, Germaine graduated and

married Carlyle, the groom chose Fred over all his old skiing and hunting buddies to be his best man, perhaps in courteous symmetry with Betsy, the matron-of-honor. He bought Fred a beige suit to match his own; the coat hung loose on Fred's narrow shoulders, and the sleeves were too long, but he felt flattered none the less. Betsy was five months pregnant, so her ceremonial dress, of royal-blue silk, was too tight. Between them, they joked it came out even. So young, they were already launched on creating another generation.

A strange incident clouded this wedding, foreshadowing trouble to come. Carlyle and Germaine were married in New Hampshire, at a summer lodge beyond Franconia belonging to Carlyle's family, and with sentimental associations for him. The Terwilliger parents were getting a divorce at the time and were too unorganized to insist on having the event on their territory, in northwestern Connecticut. With the noon hour set for the service drawing closer, Carlyle disappeared, and it was reported that he was taking a bath down at the dam – an icy little pond in the woods, created every summer by damming a mountain trickle. Mrs Terwilliger, rendered distraught by this apparent additional defection – her own husband was not present, having been forbidden to come if he brought his youthful mistress – appealed to Fred to go down and fetch the groom. Fred supposed that in his role of best man he could not shy from this awkward duty. In his black shoes and floppy new suit – double-breasted, with those wide Fifties lapels, and a white rosebud pinned in one of them – he walked down the dirt road to the dam. His

fingers kept testing his right-hand coat pocket to see if the wedding ring was still there – its adamant little weight, its cool curved edge. The road was really two dusty paths beside a central mane of weeds and grass, shadowed even toward noon by hemlocks and birches. Bears supposedly lived in these woods, which stretched endlessly, gloomily in every direction, claustrophobic as a cave. Suppose Carlyle had fled! Suppose he had gone crazy, and with his excessive, careless strength would knock his best man unconscious!

Carlyle was coming up the road, in his identical beige suit, his long wet hair combed flat, his ritual bachelor ablutions at last completed. Fred was relieved; he had been afraid of, among other things, seeing his soon-to-be brother-in-law naked. The road slanted down, to the creek, so their heads for a moment were on the same level, and in this moment Carlyle gave Fred, or Fred happened to catch, a look, a watery warm-eyed look. What did it mean? *Get me out of this*? Or was the look just a flare, a droplet, of the wordless pagan wisdom that brothers somehow shared?

'They sent me after you.'

'I see that, Freddy.'

Carlyle's eyes were an uncanny pale green, with thin pink lids, and prominent, so that his long face gave the impression of being a single smooth tender surface, his nose so small as to be negligible. When he looked intent, as now, his eyes went flat across the top, the upper eyelid swallowing its own lashes.

In the years to come, the brothers-in-law looked each other in the eyes rather rarely. Not that they lacked occasion: 71

though they lived, with their wives and children, in separate towns, and eventually on different coasts of the continent, Carlyle saw to it that they all spent at least several weeks of the year as one family. There was the Franconia place at first, and when Carlyle's mother, widowed early by a heart attack that carried off his father – the Saughterfields had fragile hearts – sold it, there were summer houses rented jointly, or two rented side by side, or Christmases spent in one or the other's home, the floor beneath the tree heaped embarrassingly high with the presents for their combined children. There were nine children, in the end: Fred and Betsy's three, Carlyle and Germaine's six. Six! Even in those years before ecology-mindedness, that was a lot, for non-Catholics. Fred and Betsy speculated that, his own father dying so young and his mother remarrying and moving to Paris (her new husband worked for American Express), Carlyle was afraid of running out of family; his New Hampshire cousins depressed him and his only sibling was a much older sister whom he never mentioned, and who lived in Hawaii with an alcoholic jerk of a husband.

The Emmets sometimes found the joint vacations heavy going. Their children were outnumbered two to one and everyone was benevolently bullied into expeditions – to the beach, to an amusement park, to some mountain trail – whose ultimate purpose seemed to be to create photo opportunities for Carlyle. He had become a fervent photographer, first with Nikons and then with Leicas, until he discovered that an even more expensive camera could be bought – a Hasselblad. Its chunky shutter sound sucked them up, sealed them in, captured them in sunshine and rain, parkas and bathing suits, the boys in their baseball caps and the girls in their ribbons and braids. One cherished photo, turned into the Saughterfields' Christmas card, showed all nine children squeezed into the Emmets' old workhorse of a Fairlane station wagon, each hot little grinning face smeared by an ice-cream cone. What the photo did not show was the drive away from the ice-cream stand: the cones melted too rapidly in the August heat and had to be thrown out the window when they became, in the mass of flesh, impossibly liquid. 'Over the side!' Carlyle called from behind the wheel, and an answering voice would pipe, 'Over the side!' and another gob of ice cream would spatter on the receding highway, to gales of childish glee. Conspicuous waste pained Fred, but seemed to exhilarate Carlyle.

As it worked out, Carlyle was often driving Fred's cars, and commandeering Betsy's kitchen for meals he would cook, dirtying every pan. He made the Emmets feel squeezed, not least with his acts of *largesse* – plastic-foam boxes of frozen steaks that would arrive before a visit, mail-ordered from Omaha, and heavy parcels of post-visit prints, glossily processed by a film laboratory in West Germany that Carlyle used. All these fond, proprietary gestures, Fred felt, spelled power and entitlement. Even taking the photographs placed Carlyle on a level above them, as an all-seeing appropriator of their fleeting lives.

Once, on Martha's Vineyard, when Fred needed his car to get to a tennis date in Chilmark and Carlyle had taken it up to Oak Bluffs to buy his daughters and nieces elephant-hair 73 bracelets, and then to Vineyard Haven for the matinee of a Jerry Lewis movie, with miniature golf on the way home, Fred let his temper fly. He felt his face flush; he heard his shrill voice flail and crack. Carlyle, who had returned from his long expedition with bags of farmstand vegetables, pounds of unfilleted fish, and a case of imported beer, stared at Fred with his uncanny green eyes for some seconds and then cheerfully laughed. It was a laugh of such genuine, unmalicious, good-tempered amusement that Fred had to join in. Through his brother-in-law's eyes he saw himself clearly, as a shrill and defensive pipsqueak. It was, he imagined, this sort of honest illumination – his sort of brusque restoration to one's true measure – that siblings offer one another. As an only child, Fred had never been made to confront his limits.

In bed he asked Betsy, 'Why does he need to do it – all this playing Santa Claus?'

'Because,' she answered, 'he doesn't have enough else to do.'

What Carlyle did professionally became vaguer with the years. After business school there had been business – putting on a suit in the morning, working for other men, traveling in airplanes to meet with more men in suits. One company he worked for made fine leather goods – purses, belts, aviator-style jackets as items of high fashion – and another a kind of machinery that stamped gold and silver foil on things, on books and photograph albums and attaché cases and such. Neither job lasted long. Carlyle's weakness, perhaps, was his artistic side. His Harvard major had been not economics but fine arts; he took photographs and bought expensive art books so big no shelves could hold them; he could not be in his house, or the Emmets', a minute without filling the air with loud music, usually opera. When his mother's sudden death – she was hit by a taxi in Paris, on the Boulevard St-Germain – brought him some additional money, he became a partner in an avant-garde furniture store in the Back Bay: chairs and tables of molded plastic, sofas in the form of arcs of a circle, waterbeds. The store did well – it was the Sixties, there was plenty of money around, and plenty of questing for new lifestyles – but Carlyle got bored, and became a partner in a Los Angeles firm that manufactured kinetic gadgets of Plexiglas and chemical fluids. This firm went bust, but not before Carlyle fell in fatal love with California – its spaghetti of flowing thruways, its pink and palmy sprawl, its endless sunshine and perilous sense of being on the edge. He moved his growing family there in 1965. As his children grew and his hair thinned, Carlyle himself seemed increasingly on the edge – on the edge of the stock market, on the edge of the movie industry, on the edge of some unspecified break-through. His clothes became cheerfully bizarre – bell-bottom pants, jackets of fringed buckskin, a beret. His name appeared as co-producer of a low-budget film about runaway adolescents (seen romantically, roving against the night lights of Hollywood and sleeping in colorful shacks up in the canyons) that received favorable reviews back east and even turned up in the Coolidge Corner movie complex not far from where Fred and Betsy lived in Brookline.

Fred, unromantically, worked in real estate. After splitting off from the management company that trained him, he bet his life on the future of drab, run-down inner-city neighborhoods that, by the sheer laws of demographics and transportation, had to come up in the world. His bet was working, but slowly, and in the meantime the Emmet Realty Corporation absorbed his days in thankless maintenance and squabbles with tenants and the meticulous game, which Fred rather enjoyed, of maximizing the bank's investment and thereby increasing his own leverage. That is, twenty thousand of his own equity, plus a hundred-thousand-dollar mortgage, meant a profit of two hundred per cent if the building's worth climbed by a third. He was, like many only children, naturally meticulous and secretive, and it warmed him to think that his growing personal wealth was cunningly hidden, annually amplified by perfectly legal depreciation write-offs, in these drab holdings – in Dorchester three-deckers and South End brick bowfronts, in asphalt-shingled Somerville duplexes and in Allston apartment buildings so anonymous and plain as to seem ownerless. He was the patient ant, he felt, and Carlyle more and more the foolish grasshopper.

Yet, when, ten years into his marriage, Fred found himself swept up in a reckless romance, it was his brother-in-law that he confessed to. The seethe of his predicament – Betsy's innocence, and the children's, and the other woman's; glittering detached details of her, her eyes and mouth, her voice and tears, her breasts and hair – foamed in him like champagne overflowing a glass. It was delicious, terrible; Fred had never felt so alive. One muggy July afternoon he found himself alone with Carlyle in the ramshackle Chatham house that the Saughterfields and the Emmets were jointly renting.

The wives and children were at the beach. Carlyle came into the living room, where Fred was working up some figures, and sat himself stolidly down opposite the desk, on the sandy, briny green fold-out sofa that came with the house. Carlyle had put weight on his big bones, and moved now with the deliberation of someone considerably older than his brother-in-law. Tennis and worry had trimmed Fred down, given him an edge – for the first time in his life, he felt handsome. Carlyle was wearing a kind of southern-California safari suit, a loose cotton jacket with matching pants, suggesting pajamas or a doctor's antiseptic outfit when he operates. He sat there benignly, immovably. To relieve the oppressive silence, Fred began to talk.

As Carlyle listened, his eyes went watery with the gravity of the crisis; yet his remarks were gracefully light, even casual. 'Well, Freddy – if I could see you with the woman, I might say, "What the hell, go to it,"' he pronounced at one point in his reedy voice, and at another point he likened the sexual drive to an automobile, volunteering of himself, 'I know it's in there, in the garage, just raring to be revved up.'

Though Carlyle seemed, if anything, to advise that Fred follow his heart ('My doc keeps telling me we only live once'), and with his noncommittal calmness did relieve his brother-in-law's agitation and guilt, Fred was left with the impression that it would be absurd of him to leave the children and Betsy and the share of the Emmet Corporation her lawyers would demand. Would Carlyle, if he ever *did* see him with the other woman, be enough impressed? Was not erotic passion in truth as mechanical as an internal-combustion engine? Perhaps, in giving him reason to talk of her to Carlyle, to brag, as it were, to the older, taller, stronger man of his conquest, the other woman had served much of her purpose. Looking back, years later, Fred wondered if the sisters hadn't known more than they seemed to, and hadn't urged Carlyle to come and have this brotherly consultation, there in the empty Chatham house sticky with salt air.

The marriages, and the families, went on. So many outings, to build up their children's childhood – beaches, mountains, shopping malls, Disney World. So much shared sunshine. Why, then, did Fred's scattered memories of Carlyle tend to be shadowy? One Christmastime in Brookline, Fred, responding to a ruthless battering sound from below, went into his cellar and discovered his brother-in-law, sinisterly half-lit by the fluorescent tubes above the workbench, pounding something glittering gripped in the vise. The other man's eyes, looking up and squinting with the change of focus, had that watery, warm – was it sheepish? – look they had worn that day of his wedding, as he came up the shady road beneath the hemlocks and birches. 'Santa's workshop,' he explained huskily. He hid with his body what he was doing. He looked demonic, or damned, in the flickering basement light. Fred backed up the stairs, as embarrassed as if he had surprised the other man undressed.

Betsy explained it to him later, in bed. To save money, Carlyle was making some of their Christmas presents this year – silver dollars drilled through and beaten into rings for
78 the boys, and strung into necklaces for the girls. It was the

sort of thing he used to do as a boy; he had been creative, artistic. It was sweet, Betsy thought.

To Fred, even this exercise in thrift savored of extravagance – silver dollars! 'Are they that hard up?' he asked. 'What's happened to all Carlyle's money?' He had always resented it that Carlyle had simply *had* money, whereas he had had to make it, a crumb at a time.

Well, according to what Betsy had gathered from Germaine, who out of loyalty of course didn't like to say much, six children in private schools and colleges aren't cheap, and the stock market had been off under Nixon, and Carlyle had trouble trimming his expensive tastes – the MG convertible, the English suits ordered tailor-made from London even though he rarely wore suits, the beach house in Malibu in addition to their seven-bedroom Mission-style home in Bel Air. The people he dealt with expected him to have these things.

'Who *does* he deal with?' Fred asked.

'*You* know,' Betsy said, in the voice of one who didn't exactly know, either. 'Movie people. He's involved in a movie now, Germaine did allow, that's just *sucking* the money out of him. He's in with this guy, Lanny somebody, who was supposed to make a low-budget blue movie with an adventure theme as well, so it would not just be for the triple-X theaters but could get into the softer-core drive-ins, but who without asking or telling Carlyle went and rented one of those sound stages that cost twenty-five thousand a day or something fantastic for these episodes that don't exactly tie in yet, since he doesn't have a real script, it's all in his head. He 79 even bought an old frame house somewhere and burned it down for one scene. Germaine thinks Carlyle is being taken for a *hor*rible ride but is too proud to say anything. You remember, all that buddy-buddy skiing and hunting he used to do? – those people used to take advantage of him, too. He has this old-fashioned sense of honor and can't defend himself. He gets caught up in a macho sort of thing. Furthermore, he likes being around these movie people, especially the little porno starlets. She wishes *you'd* talk to him.'

'Me? What would I say?' Fred's stomach pinched, there in the dark. He was still afraid of Carlyle, slightly – those flat-lidded eyes, the way he could throw a ball that made your hands hurt.

'Just open the subject. Let him tell you how it is.'

'The tried-and-true talking cure,' he said bitterly. A decade later, he still missed the woman he had given up – dreamed of her, in amazing, all-but-forgotten detail. He would never love anyone that much again. He had come to see that the heart, like a rubber ball, loses bounce, and eventually goes dead. He did feel a faint pity, smelling his brother-in-law's pain in the house. There had been a physical deterioration as well as a financial. Carlyle's doctor had told him to take afternoon naps, and it seemed he was often upstairs, in a kind of hibernation, from which he would emerge red-eyed, wearing soft moccasins. To his counterculture clothes his health problems had added a macrobiotic diet, and the clothes hung loose on his reduced, big-boned frame.

One day between Christmas and New Year's, when all the others had gone ice-skating on the Brookline Reservoir, Fred walked into the kitchen, where Carlyle was heating water for a cup of herbal tea, and asked, 'How's it going?'

The other man wore an embroidered green dashiki hanging loose outside dirty old painter pants. His hair had vanished on top, and he had let it grow long at the back; with the long graying wisps straggling at the nape of his neck, he seemed a dazed old woman, fussing at her broth. His bare arms looked white and chilly. Years in California had thinned his blood. Fred said, 'If you'd like to borrow a sweater, I have plenty.'

'Actually, I just turned up the thermostat.' Carlyle looked over at him mischievously, knowing that thrifty Fred would resent this, and continued his aggressive tack. 'Everything's going great,' he said. 'Life's all *samsara*, Freddy. The Terwilliger girls may have been stirring you up about this particular film project I have in the works, but, like they say, no sweat. It's money in the bank. When you bring your gang out this summer, we should have a rough print to show you.'

'That would be nice,' Fred said. To be brotherly, he was wearing the ring Carlyle had given him; its roughly pounded edges scratched his skin, and an inspection of the basement had disclosed that a number of his drill bits, meant for wood and not silver alloy, had been ruinously dulled.

The film, when they saw it that June in LA, also seemed crudely made. The young flesh, photographed in too hard a light, in rooms rented by the hour, had a repulsive sheen, a smooth falseness as of tinted and perfumed candles. The adventure parts of the film failed to link up. The burning house was on the screen only a few garish, orange seconds. Fred was struck by the actors' and actresses' voices, recorded with a curious flat echo that made him realize how filtered, how trained, the voices in real movies are. Carlyle's profile had been fascinating in the dark, the screen's bright moments glittering in the corner of his eye. When the lights came on, his tender-skinned face was flushed. He said sheepishly to his in-laws, 'Hope it wasn't too blue for you.'

'Maybe not blue enough,' Fred allowed himself to say. It was the nearest to a negative word he had ever dared, since that time on the Vineyard when Carlyle had laughed at his pipsqueak indignation.

Now it was his turn to be amused, when, at dinner afterwards, over Hawaiian drinks and Chinese food, while the wives held tensely silent, Carlyle hoped aloud that Fred would consider investing in the film, toward distribution and advertising costs, which were all that was left to get the package off the ground. One more boost and the movie would make everybody a bundle. He could offer eighteen per cent annual interest, just like MasterCard in reverse, or up to a quarter of the net profits, depending on how many hundred thousand Fred could see his way clear to invest. Plus, he promised, he would pay Fred's principal back right off the top, before he even paid himself. He knew Boston real estate had been going through the roof lately and Fred must be desperate for a little diversification.

Carlyle's mien, in the shadowy restaurant with its guttering hurricane lamps and pseudo-Polynesian idols, wasn't easy to read; his strained-sounding voice, almost inaudible, wheezed on doggedly, and a watery fixation glazed over the old glint – the guilty glance from the bottom of something – that Fred had caught or imagined on the hemlock-shaded road twenty-five years before.

Fred didn't laugh. He said he would think about it and talk it over with Betsy. Naturally, she had a stake in all his business decisions and was always consulted. In private he asked her, 'How important is it to you as a sister, if this would bail Germaine out?'

She said, 'It isn't, and I don't think it would anyway.'

Fred felt contaminated by the other man's naked plea, and could hardly wait until he got away, safely back to his own coast. He was too cowardly to turn Carlyle down himself. He left it to the Terwilliger sisters, Betsy to Germaine via long-distance telephone, to pass him the word: No way. Fred Emmet, too, could give a brotherly lesson in limits.

When Carlyle Saughterfield, less than a decade after his failed film had emptied his pockets, died, it was in a movie theatre. The girl next to him – not a date; they had just been introduced – noticed him at one point softly thumping his own chest, and when the lights went up the tall man was slumped as if asleep. Impassive. Wearing a green dashiki, and not much older than his father had been.

Germaine and he, some years before, had gotten divorced, and Fred and Betsy, too, as the Terwilliger sisters continued their lives in parallel. Betsy had never really forgiven him for the insult of that old affair. Germaine, a week after Betsy had phoned Fred with the stunning news, called him herself to invite him to a pagan ceremony, a scattering of Carlyle's 83 ashes in a tidal creek north of Boston where the dead man used to sail and swim as a boy.

This scattering had been his idea, as was Fred's being invited. Germaine said, 'He loved you,' which sounded right, since families teach us how love exists in a realm above liking or disliking, coexisting with indifference, rivalry, and even antipathy. What with his health troubles, ominous family history, and nothing much else to do, Carlyle had done a lot of thinking about his own death: from beyond the grave, it appeared, he was trying to arrange one more group photo. The children were adult and dispersed, most on the coasts but one in Chicago and another in New Mexico. A ragged group gathered on an appointed wooden bridge, on a February day so clear it did not feel cold.

Fred dipped his hand into the box of calcium bits that had been Carlyle's big bones and, imitating the others, carefully dropped them over the rough, green-painted rail. He had imagined that the tide would carry these fragments called ashes toward the sea, but in fact they sank, like chips of shell, tugged but not floated by the pellucid ebbing water. Sinking, doing a slow twirling dance, they caught the light. Two of Fred's nieces – young women in defiant bloom, with ruddy faces and blond hair and pale eyes flat across the top – beamed at him forgivingly, knowingly. The sunshine seemed a lesson being administered, a universal moral; it glinted off of everyone's protein strands of hair and wool hats and sweaters and chilly nailed hands and the splintered green boards of the bridge and the clustered, drifting, turning little fragments in the icy sky-blue tide. In this instant of illumination all those old photographs and those old conglomerate times Carlyle had insisted upon were revealed to Fred as priceless – treasure, stored up against the winter that had arrived.

PENGUIN 60s

MARTIN AMIS · *God's Dice*
HANS CHRISTIAN ANDERSEN · *The Emperor's New Clothes*
MARCUS AURELIUS · *Meditations*
JAMES BALDWIN · *Sonny's Blues*
AMBROSE BIERCE · *An Occurrence at Owl Creek Bridge*
DIRK BOGARDE · *From Le Pigeonnier*
WILLIAM BOYD · *Killing Lizards*
POPPY Z. BRITE · *His Mouth will Taste of Wormwood*
ITALO CALVINO · *Ten Italian Folktales*
ALBERT CAMUS · *Summer*
TRUMAN CAPOTE · *First and Last*
RAYMOND CHANDLER · *Goldfish*
ANTON CHEKHOV · *The Black Monk*
ROALD DAHL · *Lamb to the Slaughter*
ELIZABETH DAVID · *I'll be with You in the Squeezing of a Lemon*
N. J. DAWOOD (TRANS.) · *The Seven Voyages of Sindbad the Sailor*
ISAK DINESEN · *The Dreaming Child*
SIR ARTHUR CONAN DOYLE · *The Man with the Twisted Lip*
DICK FRANCIS · *Racing Classics*
SIGMUND FREUD · *Five Lectures on Psycho-Analysis*
KAHLIL GIBRAN · *Prophet, Madman. Wanderer*
STEPHEN JAY GOULD · *Adam's Navel*
ALASDAIR GRAY · *Five Letters from an Eastern Empire*
GRAHAM GREENE · *Under the Garden*
JAMES HERRIOT · *Seven Yorkshire Tales*
PATRICIA HIGHSMITH · *Little Tales of Misogyny*
M. R. JAMES AND R. L. STEVENSON · *The Haunted Dolls' House*
RUDYARD KIPLING · *Baa Baa, Black Sheep*
PENELOPE LIVELY · *A Long Night at Abu Simbel*
KATHERINE MANSFIELD · *The Escape*

PENGUIN 60s

READ MORE IN PENGUIN

For complete information about books available from Penguin and how to order them, please write to us at the appropriate address below. Please note that for copyright reasons the selection of books varies from country to country.

IN THE UNITED KINGDOM: Please write to *Dept. JC, Penguin Books Ltd, FREEPOST, West Drayton, Middlesex UB7 0BR.*

If you have any difficulty in obtaining a title, please send your order with the correct money, plus ten per cent for postage and packaging, to *PO Box No. 11, West Drayton, Middlesex UB7 0BR.*

IN THE UNITED STATES: Please write to *Consumer Sales, Penguin USA, P.O. Box 999, Dept. 17109, Bergenfield, New Jersey 07621-0120.* VISA and MasterCard holders call 1-800-253-6476 to order all Penguin titles.

IN CANADA: Please write to *Penguin Books Canada Ltd, 10 Alcorn Avenue, Suite 300, Toronto, Ontario M4V 3B2.*

IN AUSTRALIA: Please write to *Penguin Books Australia Ltd, P.O. Box 257, Ringwood, Victoria 3134.*

IN NEW ZEALAND: Please write to *Penguin Books (NZ) Ltd, Private Bag 102902, North Shore Mail Centre, Auckland 10.*

IN INDIA: Please write to *Penguin Books India Pvt Ltd, 706 Eros Apartments, 56 Nehru Place, New Delhi 110 019.*

IN THE NETHERLANDS: Please write to *Penguin Books Netherlands bv, Postbus 3507, NL-1001 AH Amsterdam.*

IN GERMANY: Please write to *Penguin Books Deutschland GmbH, Metzlerstrasse 26, 60594 Frankfurt am Main.*

IN SPAIN: Please write to *Penguin Books S. A., Bravo Murillo 19, 1o B, 28015 Madrid.*

IN ITALY: Please write to *Penguin Italia s.r.l., Via Felice Casati 20, I-20124 Milano.*

IN FRANCE: Please write to *Penguin France S. A., 17 rue Lejeune, F-31000 Toulouse.*

IN JAPAN: Please write to *Penguin Books Japan, Ishikiribashi Building, 2-5-4, Suido, Bunkyo-ku, Tokyo 112.*

IN GREECE: Please write to *Penguin Hellas Ltd, Dimocritou 3, GR-106 71 Athens.*

IN SOUTH AFRICA: Please write to *Longman Penguin Southern Africa (Pty) Ltd, Private Bag X08, Bertsham 2013.*